The Christmas Letters

The Christmas Letters

Kathy Mowery

XULON PRESS

Xulon Press Elite
2301 Lucien Way #415
Maitland, FL 32751
407.339.4217
www.xulonpress.com

Printed in the United States of America.
Edited by Xulon Press.

ISBN-13: 9781545629284

Dedication

I dedicate my debut novel to my husband, Lloyd, and to my children, Melissa and Zachary.

Acknowledgments

To Lloyd, my incredible husband, you are my best friend and I love you very much. All of your support and love mean everything to me.

To Melissa, my beautiful daughter, your wisdom blows me away. Your encouragement is what helped me get through this. I love you so much. I can't wait to see what God does in your life. I am very proud of you.

To Zachary, my handsome son, you always have a smile. You give the best hugs and you always know when I need a laugh. I am so proud to be your Mom. I love you very much. God has amazing plans for you, so it will be exciting to see what He does in your life.

Acknowledgments

Introduction

Dear Reader,

First, thank you so much for purchasing my very first novel. I cannot begin to tell you how much fun I had writing this book. I had an amazing partner—God. He and I spoke all of the time and He is the one who made this whole process possible. I am so thankful that we serve a God who is extremely patient, loving, and knew exactly what I needed when I thought I had nothing else to give.

Frank Trask writes Christmas Letters every year to specific friends in town who need something extra for the holidays. Every January, Frank begins to pray that God will reveal who should receive a Christmas Letter and by November 1, he has his complete list. His family has always been supportive that is until three years ago when Frank had a heart attack and the Christmas Letters consumed all of his time away from his family. His daughter, Emma now thinks it's time for her Dad to retire from writing his Christmas Letters and spend more time with his family.

When Frank has an accident, Emma thinks that it is God's will for her Dad to retire from writing his Christmas Letters. However, God will challenge Frank, who has to step away from the one task he loves to do more than anything else God has ever given to him. Meanwhile, Emma will face her own challenges when she falls for the Assistant Principal, Sam Watson. God will give Emma the opportunity to try something new and to take on the responsibility to write this year's Christmas Letters. This will be a Christmas the Trask family will never forget.

Chapter 1

"Yes, Dad, I have the pumpkins," Emma said, speaking on her cell phone as she walked out the door of her condo trying to get to school on time. "Yes, I plan on dropping them off after school. Bye, Dad! I am going to be late. I have to go. Love you, too."

Getting into her car, Emma Trask took a breath, checked herself out in the rearview mirror, and turned up the heat on this cold October 31 morning. *Did they really think I would forget that today is Halloween?* I think not, she thought smiling as she backed out of her driveway in her bright yellow Volkswagen convertible and made her way to the elementary school.

Emma Trask is a striking young woman who recently celebrated her thirtieth birthday. With chocolate brown wavy hair and emerald eyes, she could easily pass for someone in their twenties. Emma didn't look or act her age which is probably why she was a very good kindergarten teacher.

One more day and I can start listening to Christmas music, she thought as she turned up the radio and proceeded to school. As she pulled into the school parking lot, a car horn caused her to look into her rear-view mirror. She saw a man in a black pickup truck waving at her. *Who is that honking at me?* Emma thought and then noticed that the truck was following her onto school property. Nervously, she continued to drive until she reached her parking spot. She looked around and noticed that the truck had not only followed her, but the stranger had pulled into an administration spot right next to hers.

Emma gazed over at the stranger who smiled at her and waved. *I have no idea who you are, mister, but clearly, we do not know each other.* Getting out of her car, Emma made her way up the stairs to her school as fast as she could.

"Excuse me," a voice called from behind her.

Ignoring the man running up after her, she continued to walk quickly toward the security of the school building.

"Excuse me," she heard again closer this time.

Then he touched her arm, causing Emma to spin around angrily and face this pushy stranger.

"I'm sorry, I didn't mean to startle you," he said. "I just wanted to tell you that you have a brake light out."

Trying to regain her composure, Emma couldn't help but notice that the stranger had deep blue eyes and a gorgeous smile.

"Thanks! I will look into it," she said as she turned away.

"You don't believe me?" he asked.

"I didn't say that, I just said that I will look into it. Now if you don't mind, excuse me, I have to get to work," Emma said impatiently.

"Me, too," the stranger with the blue eyes said with a smile. "Here, let me get the door for you."

"No thank you, I can manage," Emma insisted.

"But I insist," he said as he grabbed the door and bowed. "Ladies first."

Trying not to act impressed that a man these days would open the door for a lady, Emma walked swiftly down to the nurse's office and opened the door quickly sensing that the gentleman was watching her. Emma turned around and looked out the window to see if the stranger was following her. *If he was,* she thought, *he is in for a rude awakening.*

"What are you doing?" her Mom asked from across the room, the school nurse.

Seeing no one, Emma turned around to see her Mom, Ruth Trask, sitting on a rolling chair looking at her daughter strangely.

"Nothing," Emma said, then smiled. "Morning, Mom."

"Josh, hold still while I take your temperature," her Mom said as she turned back to her young patient.

"I hate it when you put it in my ear," Josh complained.

"Well, if you didn't squirm, I could do it quickly and it would be all over in a moment," Ruth said with a smile.

"Josh, are you feeling ill again today?" Emma asked.

"Hi, Ms. Emma, I think I have the same thing as my mom," Josh said and touched his belly.

"I see," Emma smiled.

"Yep, she was throwing up again last night and I think I caught it," Josh said shaking his head sadly.

Ruth and Emma looked at each other and smiled for they knew that Josh's mom was eight months pregnant and she occasionally got sick at night.

"I bet by the time you get home this afternoon, Josh, you and your mom will both be feeling a lot better," Emma said.

"You think so?" Josh asked hopefully.

"Yes, I do," Emma grinned as she opened the door for her favorite student. "Now get to class."

"Aren't you coming?" Josh asked.

"I'll be there in a minute," Emma answered as she watched Josh slowly walk down to her classroom.

"Mom, I have to talk to you," she said excitedly.

"Later, Emma," her Mom said as she waved toward the other students waiting for her attention. "I have a full house in here this morning."

Emma turned to see every chair and both beds were full of students.

"Mom, it's important I need to speak to you, now!" Emma insisted.

"I will see you at lunch, Emma," her Mom said firmly turning to her next patient.

Watching her Mom with the students always made Emma smile.

She walked over and kissed her Mom on top of her head, "See you then."

"Emma, do you have the pumpkins?" her Mom asked as Emma started out the door.

"Really, Mom?" Emma said, looking and sounding annoyed. "Of course, I have them."

Shaking her head, she walked quickly to her classroom.

Josh was waiting for her at the door and asked, "Ms. Emma, are you going trick or treating?"

"Yes, I am," Emma responded with a warm smile. "I'm taking my nephews with me."

"Cool, what are you going to be?" Josh asked excitedly.

"Oh, I'm not dressing up," Emma told him.

Josh looked at her like he couldn't believe what he just heard her say, "You're not dressing up? You can't go trick or treating if you don't have a costume!"

"Okay, Josh," Emma asked. "What do you think I should be for Halloween?"

Josh stopped and looked up at his teacher, studying her, then smiled and said, "Supergirl!"

"Supergirl," Emma laughed. "I like it."

Though Emma loved teaching, the morning crept by very slowly. She had a hard time concentrating. She could not get the stranger she met that morning out of her mind. *He seemed to know me,* she thought sitting down at her desk. *But I don't believe we have ever met before, or have we?* Deep in thought, she jumped when the noon bell rang.

"You okay, Ms. Emma?" Josh asked. "You looked like you saw a ghost."

Smiling and getting up from behind her desk, Emma answered, "I'm fine. I was just thinking and the bell startled me."

"You must have been thinking pretty hard to jump that high," Susie giggled and jumped imitating her.

Soon her entire class was jumping in fright.

"Alright, that's enough now," Emma said, though she could not stop smiling for she knew that their imitation of her was right on. "Quiet, please, it's time to head for the cafeteria for lunch."

As they walked down the hall, Emma could see them raising their feet up and down still imitating her. She could not get mad, though. This was the best class she had ever had. Her kids were respectful five-year-olds. She couldn't be prouder. Emma loved her class.

Each year when the school year was over, Emma would cry as she thought about those students who had moved from being a very shy child to an "I can take on the world" child. That was why she enjoyed teaching kindergarten. There was always so much change from when these kids started school to the end of the school year.

"Have fun," Emma told her class as they made their way into the cafeteria.

Spotting her mom, Emma quickly made her way through the teacher's line, grabbing a bowl of tomato soup and a bottle of water.

Sitting down next to her Mom, Emma took a sip of water and a spoonful of her soup.

"Rough morning?" her Mom asked with a smile.

"You have no idea," Emma responded, rolling her eyes dramatically.

"Actually, I do. I had five kids come in this morning with stomach aches. I think some of these kids have already gotten a hold of the Halloween candy their parents are going to be giving out tonight and they gave themselves a belly ache," her Mom told her.

"I wouldn't be surprised," Emma agreed. "My kids were bouncing off the walls and jumping all the way down here."

"I saw that and wondered why they were jumping and laughing," her Mom said.

Emma told her Mom what happened and they both laughed.

"I'm sure Josh was the instigator," her Mom said with a smile.

"He was," Emma confirmed, "but Susie jumped right in."

"Well, you do know that those two are the best of friends," laughed Ruth.

"I know," Emma smiled. "They are quite a pair!"

"It was hard to get them settled and focused," Emma told her Mom. "I am so grateful that Halloween fell on a Friday this year. I wish Halloween always fell on a Friday. The kids always have a hard time staying awake after a night of trick or treating."

As they ate their lunch, Emma and Ruth continued to talk about Halloween and how they were going to get together to make caramel apples when they got home later.

Suddenly, Emma remembered what she had wanted to tell her Mom.

"This morning as I was getting out of the car in the parking lot when this man walked up to me and told me I have a brake light out," Emma explained. "Then the gentleman walked right into the school behind me this morning."

"A man walked into the school with you this morning?" Ruth looked concerned. "Who was he and what did he want?"

"Seems he just wanted to tell me I had a brake light out. Then he said he needed to get to work and walked into the school with me," Emma explained. "Has the school hired any new teachers?"

"What did this gentleman look like?" Ruth asked.

"Well, he was tall, had dark hair, clean shaven, and he had on a white oxford long sleeve shirt, deep blue jeans, and cowboy boots," Emma said recalling the handsome stranger.

"That's Sam," Ruth smiled knowingly.

"Sam who?" Emma asked, wondering why she didn't know about this Sam person.

"Emma, you're going to like him," Ruth smiled. "He's Jennifer's new Assistant Principal."

"Well, this morning he kept honking his horn at me and when he followed me into the school parking lot, it freaked me out!" Emma said, ignoring her mother's implication she might be interested in this Sam.

"Well, when you get to our house this afternoon, have your dad check it out," Ruth suggested.

As they continued eating, Emma spotted the gentleman she had seen this morning. He was talking to her best friend, Jennifer, the principal of their school.

Elbowing her Mom, "Is that Sam?"

"Where?" Ruth asked, turning to look around.

Emma smiled as Jennifer and the handsome man made their way toward them, "Hi Jennifer, how's your day going? "A lot better now that we have a new Assistant Principal. Ladies, meet Samuel Watson. Sam meet Ruth and Elizabeth Trask," Jennifer said.

Reaching his hand out to Ruth first he said, "It's nice to see you again, Ruth."

"It's good to see you, too, Sam," Ruth smiled and then turned to Emma. "Have you met my daughter, Emma?"

Turning his attention to Emma, Sam reached over to shake Emma's hand, "It's nice to meet you, Emma."

"I see you have already met Ruth," Jennifer said.

"Yes," Ruth smiled. "Sam came by earlier to get a Band-Aid."

"Paper cuts can be brutal," Sam said holding up a bandaged finger. "Ruth you're a great nurse, I can see why the kids like you so much."

Looking directly at Emma, Sam added, "Our school is lucky to have your Mom."

"Yes, we are," agreed Emma smiling at her Mom.

"Sam, we need to eat and then you need to meet the rest of the staff," Jennifer said.

"It was nice seeing you both again," Sam said.

As they started to walk away, Sam turned around and said, "Emma, make sure you get your brake light looked at as soon as you can."

"Thank you, I will," Emma answered.

"I understand you honked at my daughter this morning and scared her," Ruth said.

"Yes, I did honk, but I did not mean to scare her," Sam said apologetically. "I am sorry, Emma, if I scared you. I just wanted you to know your brake light was out. Please forgive me."

He reached out his hand to her and Emma took it cautiously, "It's okay, Sam, thanks for telling me. I'll have my Dad look into it this afternoon."

"Great," Sam said and quickly walked back to Jennifer.

"Polite and handsome wouldn't you agree?" Ruth said as she finished up her bowl of clam chowder.

"He seems nice," Emma smiled in spite of herself.

The bell rang and Ruth and Emma went back to work. To her surprise, the afternoon did go by rather quickly and after school, Emma quickly tossed all of her things into her backpack and began to make her way out of school. She was ready for the weekend and she couldn't wait to see her nephews and take them trick or treating.

As she was opening the front door, a voice came up next to her, "Here, let me get that for you."

Seeing Sam again made Emma smile and her heart beat a little faster.

"Or would you like to get the door yourself?" he asked with a grin.

"No, by all means," Emma smiled, stepping back so he could open the door for her.

As he opened the door, they were hit with a blast of chilly air, "It is going to be cold tonight."

"Yes, it is and that is fine with me," Emma remarked. "One year, it was rather warm and it just didn't seem like Halloween."

"I take it you like the cold," Sam said.

"This time of year, it just doesn't seem like Fall if it's warm," Emma explained. "I hope Jennifer didn't work you too hard on your first day."

"Not a bit," Sam said. "But she did give me a lot of reading material for over the weekend."

"Well, have a great weekend anyway, Sam."

"You, too, Emma. I'll see you Monday," Sam said with a smile. "Oh, and Emma, don't forget to get that brake light looked at."

Waving, Emma hopped into her car and headed to her parents' home with the music turned up.

I'm actually looking forward to coming back to work Monday, she thought with a smile.

Pulling into her parents' driveway, Emma smiled when she saw her Dad unloading two hay bales out of his old red truck, which had belonged to his father, for the front porch of his Victorian style home.

Turning around when he heard her car pull in, Frank Trask yelled, "Emma, give me a hand."

"I'll come right out," she called back. "I just need to change."

"Hurry, these are heavy," her Dad called back.

Walking swiftly into her parents' home, Emma found her Mom already out of her scrubs and into her jeans and her favorite

Halloween sweatshirt. She was hovering over her stove stirring her melted caramels for the apples.

"Hi, Mom, you beat me home," Emma said.

"I wanted to get a start of the caramel apples," Ruth said.

"I have to help Dad, but when I'm done, I will come help you with the apples," Emma promised as she went in to change into her jeans, high brown boots, her rust colored sweater and white vest jacket.

She pulled her hair back into a ponytail as she opened the front door. She took a deep breath.

"There's a chill in the air," she yelled to her Dad, as she walked quickly over to help him.

"I agree," Frank said and he tossed her a pair of gloves.

She reached down and grabbed one end of a hay bale.

"How was your day?" her Dad asked as they made their way to his front porch.

"Good," she said grunting. "This is heavy!"

"I know," her Dad agreed. "That's why I asked you for help!"

Seeing he was about to sit down, Emma said, "I think, there is one more, and when we're done, I have a brake light that I need you to look at."

"Brake light?" her Dad questioned. "Are you sure?"

"That is what I was told," Emma told him as they carried the second bale to the porch.

"Who told you?" her Dad asked.

"A stranger, well, I mean Sam," Emma stuttered. "Does it matter? Just take a look, please."

Placing the last bale on the other side of her parents' front door, Emma sat down, "I am so glad we don't have as many as last year."

"Me, too, but don't tell your Mom I said that," her Dad said wiping his brow. "Now, which light is out, left or right? And who's Sam?"

"I don't know which light and Sam is our new Assistant Principal," Emma answered, trying to catch her breath.

"Jennifer must be happy to finally have some help," her Dad commented. "Get into your car and let's find out which light is out."

Walking back to her car, Emma hit the ignition button and pushed down on her brakes.

"You're right, you do have a brake light out," her Dad confirmed.

"Which one is it?" she asked. "I'll make an appointment and get it fixed."

"No," her Dad said with a sly smile. "We're going to do what I have been telling you all along. We are going to go buy you a new car."

"Dad, it's just a brake light," Emma laughed.

"True, but this car is not going to last another winter," her Dad said more seriously. "They are calling for more snow and ice this year and there is no way this little car will be able to handle it. I have been telling you since you moved back here you need to get a new car. Now is the perfect time."

"But I love my bug and if anybody needs a new car or truck it's you. Grandpa's truck is looking pretty sad. Maybe you should buy yourself a car or truck," Emma said.

"My truck runs just fine, thank you. I know that you like your car and when you were teaching in Florida, it was practical, but now you're here. So, tomorrow morning, you and I are going car shopping," Frank said firmly. "We'll look for one that is more practical for the winter weather you are going to face here."

"Fine, now can you help me get all of the pumpkins out of my car? You know, the ones you and Mom both asked me not to forget?" Emma laughed.

"I almost forgot," laughed Frank.

As Frank and Emma unloaded all of the pumpkins from her car, Emma noticed the for-sale sign on the house across the street from her parents was missing.

"Who bought the Smiley home?" she asked her Dad.

"I don't know, haven't seen the owner yet," he said.

"The home definitely needs some tender loving care," she said.

"It sure does," her Dad agreed. "How does Mom want me to lay these ten pumpkins out?"

"I don't know, but I'll go ask," Emma said, walking back into the house.

"Mom, where do you want the pumpkins?" Emma asked, taking another bite of cooked caramel.

"I don't care, but make sure the walkway is well lit," Ruth answered.

Emma walked back outside and told her Dad, "She doesn't care, but she wants us to make sure the walkway is well lit. Do you think we have enough pumpkins to make Mom happy?"

"Probably not, but I think it's you who enjoys all of the pumpkins anyway," her Dad laughed.

"Really?" Emma laughed remembering how they both reminded her to get the pumpkins earlier that morning. "Dad, why do we need so many pumpkins? If you ask me we only need two, one for each hay bale. It is going to take you a couple of hours to carve all of them."

"Did you ever think that if I am out here carving, I am out of your Mom's way?" her Dad pointed out with a knowing smile.

"I see your point," Emma said as she went back in the house to help her mother with the caramel apples.

"Mom, I'm ready to help," Emma said as she took off her jacket and rolled up her sleeves. "What can I do?"

"You can start by sticking a skewer in each apple," Ruth answered.

"How was your afternoon, Mom?" Emma asked putting on an apron.

"Pretty uneventful. How was yours?"

"Same," Emma said as she picked up an apple, shoved the skewer into the bottom, and then laid the apple on a sheet of wax paper. Continuing this process, Emma worked on the apples while her Mom melted the caramel.

"I noticed that the Smiley house sold. Do you know who bought it?" Emma asked.

"No, I don't. I'm sure we will meet them eventually," her Mom said.

"What makes you think that the home belongs to a 'them'?" Emma asked.

"Well, it would make sense. It's an awful big home for someone that is single," Ruth said. "It's a family home just like this one. In fact, the house has the same layout as this one."

"Really?" Emma asked. "How do you know that?"

"Dad and I took a tour one afternoon when they had a showing," her Mom explained. "The Smileys took care of it, but I think it was getting too much for them since their children have grown and moved away. When I spoke to Mrs. Smiley, she mentioned several times that they really wanted to move to Florida so they could be nearer to the kids and grandkids."

Emma enjoyed working with her Mom on the holiday preparations. She thought of former holidays when she was younger which led her to think about Thanksgiving and then Christmas.

"Mom," Emma said as she thought about what was coming up as they approached Christmas. "I take it we won't be seeing much of Dad again this holiday season?"

"Emma, can we get through Halloween without you hounding your Dad about his Christmas Letters?" her Mom said with a touch of annoyance in her voice.

"Is she complaining already?" her Dad said as he walked into the kitchen.

"Ask your Dad," Ruth said, smoothly passing the buck. "He's standing right there."

"Dad, is it going to be like last year?" Emma asked as she turned to her Dad. "We won't be seeing much of you after today?"

"Emma, I know where you are going with this, but, yes, I am going to be busy," her Dad said as if he had answered that question a hundred times before.

"I still don't understand why you continue to write Christmas Letters to strangers," Emma said.

"They are not strangers," he stated. "Your Mom and I know them."

"But Dad, Mom puts out a Christmas letter of her own every year, isn't that enough?" Emma asked.

"No!" her Dad said emphatically. "Those are her letters they are different from mine and you know that."

"No, I don't because you have never shared with me what you are writing or to whom," Emma replied.

"That's right because it isn't any of your business," he smiled taking the edge off his words. "Emma, these letters are important to the people who receive them."

"More important than your own family?" Emma pouted.

"You know that is not true!" Frank answered growing impatient with the conversation.

"Do I?" Emma said under her breath as she pushed another skewer into an apple. "Isn't it about time you retired?"

"Retire?" her Dad asked. "Why would I want to retire?"

"Because since your heart attack, it takes you twice as long to write those letters," Emma answered getting annoyed herself.

"As long as the Lord allows me to write, I will continue to do so. I don't want to discuss this anymore. Let's just enjoy Halloween," Frank said and left to go back outside.

Emma knew it was no use talking to Dad about his writing anymore, so she said to her Mom, "If you don't need me anymore, I think I'll go sit on the porch and wait for our guests to arrive."

"Emma, you need to enjoy today and quit thinking about tomorrow," her Mom quietly advised. "Just take one day at a time."

"I know, Mom," Emma said as she grabbed a cup of hot chocolate and planted herself on her parents' front porch swing which was more comfortable than the hay bales.

Looking up, she said, "Can't **You** make him quit?"

Emma not only loved her parents, she enjoyed spending time with them. That's what makes this time of year so difficult. Her mom, Ruth had a smile that would light up a room. Her Mom loved God, her family, and Christmas! Her Dad, a country boy who grew up in Texas, had high morals and values which he passed onto his two children, Ben, Emma's older brother and Emma.

As dusk approached, her brother and his family arrived along with Jennifer and family. This made Emma happy. Her family and her best friend were there with her, what could be better? *Oh, yeah,* she thought, *her Dad retiring from writing*.

With the kids, all inside, Jennifer and Emma made their way out to the front porch swing for a few minutes alone.

"Quiet at last," Jennifer said.

"Your boys seem excited about Halloween," Emma said.

"Jason picked them up from school because I was still on the phone with one of our parents. By the time I got home they were already in their costumes, had their candy pails in hand, and were ready to go. I asked if Mommy could just change clothes first and they both said no together as if they had rehearsed it!"

Emma and Jennifer laughed, "Like I am going trick or treating in a dress and heels!"

Taking a bite of candy they each took from the bowl by the front door, Jennifer asked, "Are you okay, Emma, you seem distracted and not in the Halloween spirit."

Jennifer knew Emma well. They were college roommates and were the best of friends. Jennifer had always been very confident and outspoken, while Emma used to be insecure and quiet. They each brought out the best in the other and by the time they graduated, Jennifer had a quieter confidence about her while Emma had a more outspoken confidence. Jennifer learned how to keep things to herself while Emma used her confidence and her outspokenness to get her first teaching job.

"If you want to be a good teacher you need to have a voice and confidence," Jennifer once told Emma.

While Jennifer figured out early that she liked being in charge, Emma showed her that she needed tact and sometimes needed to keep things to herself and not say the first thing that popped into her head. They made a good team and their friendship continued to blossom after college.

"It's Dad," Emma shared. "He's sending out his Christmas Letters again."

"Yeah, so?" Jennifer asked.

"He needs to retire," Emma snapped.

Trying not to choke on her Snickers bar, Jennifer asked, "You want your Dad to retire from writing his Christmas Letters? Emma, those Christmas Letters are important to him."

"But he needs to start spending more time with Mom," Emma argued.

"Is your Mom complaining?" Jennifer asked.

"No, and you know she won't," Emma insisted. "I'm just looking out for her."

"No, you are looking out for yourself," Jennifer said, shaking her head. "I know you are not going to like what I am about to say."

"Then don't say it!" Emma snapped, feeling annoyed with everyone.

Jennifer grabbed her friend's arm before she could walk away and asked, "Emma, have you ever thought about what giving up those letters would do to your Dad, not to mention to the ones who receive his letters?"

Pulling her arm away, Emma said angrily, "No!"

She went inside and slammed the door. Walking into the kitchen, she caught her brother's attention and gestured for him to follow her. Seeing that Jennifer had come inside and was talking to her mom, Emma pulled her brother out to the front porch.

"Emma, what's wrong?" her brother Ben asked.

Tears swelled in Emma's eyes as she told him, "Dad is going to write again."

"He writes every year," Ben pointed out, wondering what the crisis was.

"Ben, don't you miss Dad when he gets caught up in his letter writing project?" Emma asked.

"Of course, I do, but I know how much it means to him," Ben answered. "Besides, you know we can't tell Dad what to do."

"Well, I think you should try," Emma said pointedly.

"You want me to tell our Dad that he needs to stop writing his Christmas Letters? Are you kidding me?" Ben laughed as if what she was asking was a joke.

"No, I'm not joking" she shot back. "I don't see what you find is so amusing."

"Emma, when has Dad ever listened to us?" Ben asked. "The only person Dad truly listens to is Mom and he doesn't listen to her all the time either."

"That is why he needs to listen to us now!" Emma emphasized. "Last year, it took him almost two months to write all of the letters. Don't you remember how frazzled he was and how tired he got? I was afraid that he was going to have another heart attack."

Ben got quiet and then said, "I understand where you are coming from Emma, but Mom kept a close eye on him and he listened when she threatened to burn all of the paper and envelopes he had for his letters if he didn't take it easier."

"That was the only thing that made him slow down," Emma remembered.

"Emma," Ben said, "I spoke to Dad about his Christmas Letters a couple of weeks ago and he reassured me that he would take it easy this year."

"What makes you think he will?" Emma asked.

"Because I told him if he didn't, I would come over here and burn his address book, paper, and everything else I could find to keep him from writing, and not just at Christmas time either."

Emma could not help but laugh when she thought what it must have looked like when her Dad was confronted by her brother who was four inches taller than her Dad.

Just then, the front door opened and Jennifer walked out saying, "The kids are getting anxious, and Ben your wife is looking for you."

Ben hugged his sister and made his way back in the house.

"Are you still mad at me?" Jennifer asked as she handed Emma a Twix bar.

Emma accepted the peace offering and smiled, "I'm sorry, Jenn, I just don't want my Dad to have another heart attack or worse."

"I know, but you need to let him live his own life," Jennifer counseled her wisely, then dropped the subject of the Christmas Letters.

Emma owed Jennifer a lot. Jennifer had always been there for Emma and Emma for Jennifer. In fact, after Frank's heart attack when Emma came back home looking for a teaching job, Jennifer was thrilled to place her in her school. She also loved giving her best friend a hard time that she was her boss now. Emma knew what Jennifer was advising her was to help her, not hurt her. She loved her for it, though it hurt to think about what the next couple of months were going to be like.

"What do you think of Sam?" Jennifer asked.

"He seems nice," Emma answered, fully aware what Jennifer was up to.

"Nice?" Jennifer asked, fishing for more.

"Yes, he's nice," Emma said with a smile. "I would even say he's a gentleman."

"That's quite a compliment," smiled Jennifer.

"Actually, I was trying to remember when the last time a man held the door open for me," Emma said. "Does Jason hold the door for you?"

"Only when we are on a date, which is rare by the way," Jennifer said then quickly added. "So, if you are willing to babysit, we could schedule a date."

"I would love to watch your boys so you two can have a date night, but you know my schedule with the Thanksgiving pageant coming up and Christmas. I do not have the time right now, but definitely after Christmas, I'm all yours," Emma said with a smile. "Just give me a little bit of notice."

Both women laughed, enjoying the end of the momentary tension between them.

"Let's go, Aunt Emma," said Nathan, one of Emma's nephews impatiently.

"Are my boys ready, too?" Jennifer asked pretending she didn't see them behind Emma's nephew.

"We're ready, Mom!" said Jack, the eldest of Jennifer's sons.

"Okay, then go tell everybody it's time to go," Jennifer told them laughing.

The boys yelled excitedly and everyone came charging out with the Halloween buckets in hand.

"Well, I guess our quiet time is over, I'll get my coat and I will be ready," Emma said with a smile.

Ruth, Jennifer, Emma, and all of the boys started out for an evening of trick or treating. As they went house-to-house, the temperature started to drop. After a couple of hours, they could tell the boys were starting to get tired. Everything came to a head when Jack told his mom that Jonathan wanted him to carry his candy pail.

"I said no," Jack said disgustedly, "and now he is crying like a baby."

"Is his bucket full?" Jennifer asked Jack.

"Yes, but mine isn't," Jack pointed out.

"Well, between the two of you I think we have enough candy, so why don't we say good night and head home.

"But mine isn't full!" Jack complained.

"I'll tell you what Jack," Ruth said. "If you go over to my house, just tell your Dad and Mr. Frank that I said you can fill up the rest of your pail with our candy."

"I can do that?" he asked with a happy look on his face.

"Yes, you can," Ruth smiled.

"Come on, Mom," Jack said and started to cross the street.

"Wait, Jack," Jennifer yelled. "Jonathan, are you coming?"

"I'm coming," Jonathan said tiredly, dragging his Halloween bucket.

"Emma, Ruth, thanks again. I will see you both Monday morning," Jennifer said as the boys urged her across the street.

"Aunt Emma, can we go on?" Nathan asked.

"Grandma, I'm tired," said his younger brother, David.

"Aunt Emma, can you go with me to one more house?" her nephew asked.

"Sure," she smiled as they approached the house directly across the street from her parents' house.

"I don't want to go to any more houses, I'm cold," David said. "I want to go to your house, Grandma. I want hot chocolate."

"Okay, we're going home," Ruth said grabbing her grandson's hand. "Emma, you'll have to tell me who lives there."

"I will," Emma assured her as she watched her mom and her nephew cross the street to her parents' home.

"Grandpa sure did a great job on the pumpkins," Nathan remarked as he ran up the lawn to the front door of their new neighbor's house.

Knocking on the door, they waited for what seemed like forever to a child.

"Maybe they ran out of candy," Emma said. "I'll knock one more time and if they don't come, we'll head over to Grandma's, okay?"

She knocked one more time and still no answer, so she said, "Well, I guess we're done. I really wanted to meet Grandma and Grandpa's new neighbors, too."

Just as Emma and her nephew were turning around to leave, the door opened and there stood a man with a Santa Claus hat and a very ugly Christmas sweater.

"Sam!" Emma said with surprise.

They both looked shocked to see one another.

"You live here?" she asked.

"Yes, I just moved in, but what are you doing here?" he asked, pleased to see her.

"Trick or treating with my nephew," she said looking down as the boy moved in front of her.

"Trick or treat," he said shyly.

Sam knelt down and asked him, "Do you have a 'trick' for me or do you just want candy?"

"Candy, please," he said without thinking twice.

Emma and Sam laughed.

"Do you live around here?" Sam asked.

"Actually, you see that house across the street with the hay bales on the front porch?" Emma asked pointing at her parents' house.

"You mean the one with all of the pumpkins all over the front lawn?" Sam asked laughing.

"Yes, that's my parents' house," Emma explained.

"Your parents live across the street?" Sam asked. "Wow, small world. Well, if I ever get hurt, it's nice to know I have Ruth right across the street."

"Yes, it is a small world indeed," Emma agreed.

"I have to say I was curious about who was carving all of those pumpkins," Sam admitted.

"It was my Dad," Emma said proudly.

"Aunt Emma, can we go to Grandma's now," her nephew asked. "I'm cold and I want some hot chocolate."

"Yes, we can go," Emma said. "It was nice seeing you again, Sam."

"Wait, what's your name, young man," Sam asked her nephew.

He looked up at Emma for permission. They had been told to never give their names to strangers.

"It's Nathan," he said shyly after Emma nodded her head.

"Nathan, I'm Sam. I work at the school with your Aunt and your Grandma. Go ahead and take two handfuls of candy."

Nathan's eyes lit up, "Really?"

"One is enough, Nathan," Emma replied. "He and his brother have enough candy."

"I insist," Sam said, putting another handful of candy in Nathan's bag. "I bought two much as usual. Besides, they need it more than I do."

"You can bring it to school on Monday and the teachers and staff will love you for it," Emma suggested.

Leaning toward Emma's left ear, Sam whispered, "I have five more bags that have not even been opened yet."

"Great! Bring those to school Monday as well," Emma laughed.

Now, with three handfuls of extra candy in his bag, Nathan said, "Thanks, Sam!"

"You're welcome, Nathan. It was nice meeting you," Sam said shaking his hand.

"Nice meeting you, too," Nathan said as he ran down the sidewalk, stopped, and looked both ways, then crossed the street, and ran on up to his grandparents' home.

"Well, I better go," Emma said. "You have a nice home, Sam."

Emma turned to go, then turned back and said, "You know hot chocolate sounds really good, you want to come and have some hot chocolate and meet the rest of my family?"

"Sure, who doesn't like hot chocolate on a cold night like this?" Sam answered quickly.

"You want to get your coat?" Emma asked.

"This sweater is warm, so I don't need a coat," Sam said then looked at Emma's face. "You don't like my sweater, do you?"

"That is the ugliest Christmas sweater I have ever seen," she laughed. "If there was an ugly sweater contest, you would win."

"Well, it just so happens that there was a contest on who could make the ugliest Christmas sweater and I did win," he said proudly.

"You made that?" Emma asked.

"I sure did!" Sam declared and puffed out his chest.

"Wow, I'm impressed," Emma admitted sincerely. "The blinking lights are a nice touch."

"Emma, you are right about the temperature dropping, maybe I should go back and get my coat," Sam said trying to turn back inside.

"Nope, too late now," Emma laughed grabbing his arm. "Living in Florida, we never had a cold Halloween. It just doesn't seem like Fall unless it starts to get cold this time of year."

"I take it, you would prefer snow instead of the beach for Christmas?" Sam asked.

"Absolutely!" smiled Emma.

Walking up to her parents' home, Emma waved to her Dad who was sitting in the driveway by the fire pit handing out candy with her brother, Ben.

"Dad, this is Sam Watson. He moved into the Smiley home. Sam is our new Assistant Principal," Emma explained.

Frank Trask stood up and shook Sam's hand, "Welcome to the neighborhood, Sam."

"Sam, this is my brother, Ben."

Shaking his hand, Ben said, "Nice sweater, Sam."

"I made it myself," Sam said laughing.

"So, what do you think about the neighborhood?" Frank asked him.

"It's quiet and it's close to the school," Sam answered.

"I think you will like it here," Frank said. "Neighbors are friendly and we all help each other out when needed."

"I'll keep that in mind," Sam said.

"We're going to go say hello to Mom," Emma said as she opened the front door.

Ruth appeared from the kitchen when she heard the door open, "Sam, what a surprise! But where's your coat? You should know better than to be out on a night like this without a coat! What if one of the students saw you? What kind of example are you setting for them as their Assistant Principal when they see you without a coat?"

Emma just smiled.

"Ruth, I assure you this sweater is very warm. I do not need my coat," Sam said politely.

"Mom, Sam bought the Smiley house," Emma explained.

"Well, then you can easily go get your coat if you're going to sit outside," Ruth said confidently.

"Yes, Mam, I'll go get my coat," he said respectfully.

"You have bought a beautiful home, Sam," Ruth told him.

"Yes, it is. It just needs some work. I am so thankful you're living right here across the street," Sam said.

"Do you think you'll need a nurse?" Ruth asked.

"Well, when I was ten, I fell off my parents' ladder and broke my leg trying to help them with house repairs," Sam shared.

"Oh, my goodness," Ruth gasped. "We'll be sure to keep my eye on you then."

"Thanks, I appreciate that. I'll be right back," Sam told Emma, as he took off sprinting to his house to grab a coat.

As Emma watched Sam, she texted Jennifer to let her know that Sam had bought the house across the street from her parents. When he came running up the lawn, Emma snapped a picture and sent it to Jennifer before he reached the porch.

When he got up on the porch, he asked, "Why did you just take a picture of me?"

Smiling, she answered, "I have my reasons. Are you ready for a cup of hot chocolate? Oh, and you might want to put on your coat unless you want another lecture from my Mom?"

He had quickly grabbed his coat and carried it across the street, not stopping to put it on. Realizing the wisdom in Emma's suggestion, he put his coat on, while Emma went to get the hot chocolate. Then Emma and Sam made their way to the porch swing.

"Your parents are great," Sam said, sipping his hot chocolate. "They remind me of my parents, always leaning on each other. I'll be happier when they get here. I miss them."

"They don't live near here?" Emma asked, wrapping her hands around her mug.

"No, they live in Phoenix," Sam answered.

"When was the last time you saw them?" Emma asked, remembering what it was like to live in Florida with her parents here.

"July fourth," Sam told her. "I flew back for a couple of weeks before I headed here to look for a job."

"Once, my parents went on a fifteen-day cruise and I hated it," Emma confessed. "Don't get me wrong, I'm glad they had fun. It was just not hearing from them that I didn't like. They had no cell coverage on most of the cruise."

Beginning to feel the chill, they decided to head over to the fire pit.

"Had you been looking for a job long?" Emma asked.

"No, I had just finished up the school year back home as a teacher at the high school," Sam said.

"What did you teach?" Emma asked.

Taking another sip of hot chocolate, Sam said, "US History, which was fun as long as we got to go on field trips."

"You didn't like teaching?" Emma asked.

"I love teaching. I just didn't like being stuck in a classroom all day long. Then I got a phone call from Peter Trust. Do you know Peter Trust?"

"Yes," Emma said. "He's been with the school district a long time."

"Well, he and my Dad are good friends. They went to college together. Sometime last year, he and my Dad were talking and Dad mentioned to him that I wanted to get back into Administration. So, I flew out here a couple of times, interviewed for, and was offered the principal position at the new high school when it opens up next Fall."

"Wow! That's exciting, Sam," Emma said.

"I'm pretty excited about it. So, in the meantime, Peter put me here to help Jennifer out until her former assistant comes back from maternity leave which I think will be right after the holidays," Sam explained. "Then I'll be heading over to the high school to assist the principal and help out until next year, which means as soon as the holidays are over, I'll be leaving."

"Don't let the staff hear you talk like that, you'll hurt their feelings," Emma said.

"Oh, I didn't mean that the way it sounded," Sam said.

Emma laughed, "I know, I just wanted to see your reaction. So, when will you see your parents again?"

They are coming for Thanksgiving and they'll stay through Christmas," Sam said with a smile. "That means that I need to get my house in order and decorated. My Mom loves Christmas and the more decoration and lights you have the better."

"My Mom is the same way," Emma said. "She will start Christmas shopping and decorating tomorrow."

"Tomorrow? November first?" he said shocked. "That's a bit early isn't?"

"Not for my Mom," Emma grinned.

Getting up, Sam said, "It's getting late and you're cold."

"Yes, I am," Emma admitted.

"So, I will say good night. Thank you, Emma," Sam said handing his mug to her, "for asking me to join you and your family tonight for hot chocolate. This has been one of the best Halloweens I've had in a very long time."

"It was fun for me, too," Emma said sincerely. "Good night, Sam. I will see you Monday morning."

"Yes, you will," Sam said as he headed back to his home.

As Sam walked across the street, Emma smiled and for the first time in a long time she could not wait until Monday.

As Emma made her way back into her parents' home, she saw her mom and her nephews separating the candy the boys had received.

"Where's Dad?" she asked.

Her Mom pointed toward her Dad's office. Emma knocked and walked in.

"Long list this year?" she asked with a frown.

"Not at all," her Dad said smiling. "Only ten Christmas Letters this year."

Surprised, Emma asked, "That's less than last year, right?"

"Yes, it is," Frank said. "I can see your wheels turning, though, Emma."

"Why do you have to start so early on the Christmas Letters if you only have ten?" she asked.

"I have to start now or I won't get them finished for Christmas," her Dad told her. "I promised Ben I would take it easy this year so I don't get so tired."

"Dad, ten letters should not take you that long," Emma suggested. "Besides, Thanksgiving is still a month away and then another month until Christmas."

Holding up his right hand to stop his daughter, "I can't wait that long and you know it. It takes time and preparation for all that I do."

"Well, maybe you should retire from writing them," Emma suggested.

"I have a responsibility to these people who need to hear from me," Frank said firmly.

"You have a responsibility to your family, too," she pouted.

"Emma, you know I do it every year and still you insist on trying to tell me what I should and should not do. I do take care of my family," Frank said getting annoyed. "I would really appreciate it if you would stop interfering and respect my decision."

It was no use talking to her Dad anymore about his Christmas Letters. His mind was made up and Emma knew that her family would not see much of her Dad until Christmas Eve. This saddened Emma to the point that she almost started to cry.

She turned away and started to walk out the door when her Dad spoke, "Emma, when you're not so emotional, I will share with you why I write them."

"I am ready now," Emma said.

"No, you're not. It's been a long day and you are tired. I will see you in the morning. We are going car shopping, right?"

Emma couldn't help but smile, "Okay, Dad. See you in the morning."

Giving her Dad a hug, "I will see you in the morning, ten o' clock okay?"

"Ten is fine, but don't be late," he grinned.

Walking back into the kitchen, Ruth spotted Emma "It's okay, Emma," Ruth said, hugging her daughter.

Nothing ever got passed Ruth. She knew her daughter very well.

"No luck," Emma said shaking her head sadly.

She hugged everyone goodbye and made her way to her car.

Getting into her old Volkswagen, she said, "Come on girl, one more night."

Emma cranked up the heat and turned up her radio. All the way home Emma thought about what her Dad said to her. Jennifer had told her to let her Dad live his own life. Ben had asked her what the Christmas Letters meant to those who receive them. Her Mom had asked her to respect her Dad's decision.

Suddenly, Emma's stomach started to turn. *No, I am not going there*, she said to herself. Turning up the music even louder, Emma sang all the way home as she forced herself to get into the Christmas spirit.

Chapter 2

The next morning, Emma walked into her kitchen and made herself a cup of coffee as she did every morning. Then she sat in the window seat in the living room of her condo seeing it was another beautiful bright sunny day. When she finished her coffee, Emma got herself ready to go buy a new car. Getting in and starting her car, she checked herself out in mirror.

"Well, old girl, this is it. You have been very dependable, but it is time for an upgrade."

She turned up the music which was now Christmas music and headed to her parents' home. Driving past Sam's house and turning into the driveway of her parents' home put a smile on her face. *Today, I am buying a car,* she said to herself. She checked herself out in her rearview mirror one last time.

As she got out of her car, Emma gave a quick glance over at Sam's house and noticed his garage was open. Walking up to her parents' front door, she could see that all of the front lawn pumpkins had already been picked up. The only ones left were on the hay bales. Her Mom had been busy already!

"Hello," she yelled from the front door.

"In here, Emma," called her mother from the kitchen.

She could tell her mom was baking, but she didn't know what.

"What are you baking, Mom? It smells wonderful in here!"

"Pumpkin pies," her Mom said with a smile. "Why do you think your Dad buys so many pumpkins? He knows I will not throw them away."

"So, how many pies are you baking?" Emma asked.

"Six. I'm taking four to the church luncheon tomorrow," her Mom explained.

"Is Dad in his office?" Emma asked.

"Yes. You two have fun," her Mom said with a big smile.

"Thanks, Mom. When we get back, I'll want a piece of pie," Emma said, licking her lips in anticipation.

Emma walked to her Dad's office, knocked, and walked in. "Hi, Dad, are you ready to go?"

"I am," he said happily. "And when we are done, I would like to drop by the post office. I need to get some Christmas stamps."

"Dad, don't you get tired of writing to people you barely know?"

"No. Emma, and we're done talking about this. Now let's go!"

Getting into her car, her Dad asked, "Do you know you what kind of car of you want?"

"Yes, I did some research last night," Emma said with a secretive smile.

"Great, so where are we headed?" her Dad asked.

"It's a surprise," Emma said as she turned up her Christmas music.

Emma and her Dad started to sing, "It's the Most Wonderful Time of the Year."

"This is my favorite song," Frank said with a smile. "Your Mom's, too."

Pulling into the local Jeep dealer, Emma stopped her car and smiled.

"I should have known," her Dad said excitedly. "Let's go pick out a car."

Walking around the parking lot, it didn't take long for Emma to find her new car—a black Jeep Cherokee.

"This is what you want?" her Dad asked with a smile of approval.

When she said a definitive, "Yes," they went in and finished all of the paperwork.

Then they jumped into Emma's new car and headed to the post office.

"Do you want to come in?" he asked her.

"No, I'll wait here," Emma said with a smile.

"I'll be back in a minute," Dad said.

Emma shook her head thinking, *I can't wait until he quits writing these Christmas Letters.*

After looking at her owner's manual and trying out every button on her dashboard, Emma thought about going after her Dad. It seemed like he had been gone quite a while. When she was about to open her car door to go look for him, her Dad came out and got in the car.

"I'm sorry Emma," he said. "I ran into someone from church."

"I was wondering what was taking you so long," Emma said as she pulled out of the parking lot and headed back to her parents' home.

"See you later, Emma," her Dad said as he went into his office as soon as they got home.

Emma headed into the kitchen where her Mom was putting the last pie into the oven.

"Did you buy a car?" her Mom asked.

"Sure did," Emma said with a big smile. "It's sitting out there in the driveway."

"I'll have to go look at it when I'm done in here," her Mom said with a smile. "You look like you could use a piece of pie, though."

"It's that obvious?" Emma asked.

"I bet you tried to talk your Dad out of writing his Christmas Letters, again," her Mom said knowingly. "You get the same look on your face every year when you don't get your way."

"I just don't understand why he keeps writing them," Emma said shaking her head.

"You don't have to understand, but you do have to respect his wishes," her Mom told her firmly.

"Don't you get tired of Dad not being around much during the holidays?" Emma asked.

"I miss his company at times, but it lets me get my things done for the holidays, too," Ruth answered. "I also know why he is writing them."

"You do?" Emma asked. "Then please tell *me*!"

"It is not my place to tell you," her Mom said shaking her head. "If your Dad wants you to know, he will be the one to tell you."

"So, you're on his side, then," Emma said with a deep sigh.

"It has nothing to do with sides," her Mom said. "Would you like a glass of milk with your pie?"

"Yes, please," Emma answered. "I'm sorry, Mom. It's just that I miss Dad."

"I know," Ruth said kindly. "But he is doing this for a very good reason. You trust him, right?"

"Of course, I trust him," Emma said.

"Then respect his wishes," her Mom said firmly.

"Alright, I will try," Emma agreed.

"Now, I need to get going," Ruth said taking off her apron. "I have some shopping to do. I will see you tomorrow at church."

Walking out with her Mom to show her the new car, she spotted Sam's truck in his driveway. She gave her Mom a hug and kiss and then decided to pay Sam a visit. Driving across the street seemed silly, but Emma wanted to show off her new car. Walking up to his front door, Emma knocked but there was no answer. She knocked again thinking maybe he was busy. Just when she was about to give up, Sam opened his door. He was dressed in jeans, a hoodie, and work gloves.

"Good morning, Emma," he said warmly.

"I was wondering if you would like to go for a ride in my new car," Emma explained.

Peeking around Emma at the new Jeep sitting in his driveway, he said, "You don't waste any time, do you?"

"Not when my dad tells me we are buying a new car," she said as they both laughed. "So, how about a ride?"

"I would, but well look at me," Sam said. "I don't want to get your new car filthy."

"You do look pretty dirty," Emma agreed, wanting to ask what he was doing, but thinking it wasn't any of her business.

"How about a rain check?" Sam asked.

"Sounds good," Emma answered trying not to show her disappointment.

"Okay, then I will see you Monday morning," Sam said.

As Emma started to walk away, Sam said, "You know I could use some help if you are not busy."

Curious, she asked, "Help you with what exactly?"

"I'm raking leaves and trying to clean up the backyard," he explained. "It seems the previous owners gave attention to the front yard, but not much to the back."

"Raking leaves? No thank you," Emma said shaking her head. "I did my share when I lived at home. If you ask me, it is a big waste of time. As soon as you're done, more leaves fall from the trees and it never gets done."

"I'll make hot chocolate afterwards," Sam pleaded. "I could really use the help!"

"Well, if there is hot chocolate involved, how can a girl refuse?" Emma said with a laugh.

"Great, follow me," Sam said leading the way through his house. "Excuse the mess. I'm still trying to get everything unpacked."

"Looks like you have done quite a bit already," Emma said looking around his home curiously.

Noticing the huge fish tank along the back wall, Emma stopped and said, "Wow! Now this is impressive!"

"Yeah, these guys keep me calm after a day at the office," Sam said with a smile.

"I'm sure they do!" Emma agreed.

"Do you have any pets?" Sam asked Emma.

"No, I'm allergic to cats and I really do not have the time nor am I home enough to have a dog."

"That's why I have a fish tank," Sam explained. "No fuss!"

"Really?" Emma said staring at the fish tank. "I don't know a lot about fish, but I do know you have to clean the tank and you do have to feed them."

"Do you have someone to clean the tank?" Emma asked wondering who that someone could be.

"Yes, just when I am traveling," Sam said, then asked, "Now, shall we head out to the back yard?"

Moving along his kitchen, Emma was not only impressed with Sam's house, they both seem to have the same kind of taste.

Walking into his backyard, Emma exclaimed, "Wow! I forgot how big these back yards are!"

"Isn't your parents' yard just as big?" Sam asked.

"I guess so, but I haven't been in my parents' back yard in a while," Emma explained.

"Your parents don't use their back yard?" Sam asked.

"Not really," Emma answered. "The only ones who really use it are my nephews. When I was a kid we did, but now they mainly use their front yard. In fact, I think their front yard is bigger than the back yard."

"Well, this is a huge back yard and I really need to get these leaves raked," Sam said handing Emma a rake and gloves.

"So, why did you buy such a big house, if you don't mind me asking?" Emma asked. "The people who lived here before had four kids and a dog, so I can see why they bought it. But you're single, right?" Emma realized she was assuming he was single. "I mean, you're not wearing a ring, so...."

"Yes, Emma," Sam said with a smile, "I'm single."

It took them a couple of hours, but when they were done, Sam's back yard looked bigger and better than it did before.

"Well, what do you think?" Sam asked, pleased with what they had accomplished.

"I think that the next time you need to rake your back yard, go ask my Dad for his riding mower," Emma said as she pulled off her gloves.

"So, noted," Sam answered, "Thank you for helping me out. I really appreciate it. Ready for some hot chocolate?"

Sam led the way back into his home, "I can make coffee if you prefer."

"No, hot chocolate is fine. In fact, I prefer it to coffee," Emma told him.

"I thought all of you teachers loved your coffee morning, noon, and night," Sam laughed.

"I do enjoy a cup of coffee in the morning, but after that, it's hot chocolate!" Emma said.

"But if you don't have hot chocolate, coffee will do," she added.

"I have hot chocolate," Sam said. "And once you have had my hot chocolate, you'll want the recipe."

As Sam made the hot chocolate, Emma scoped out Sam's living room. She looked at his fish and admired the pictures he had around and on the wall.

One painting in particular caught her eye, "This manger scene is beautiful!"

"Thanks, it's one of my favorites," Sam said. "My Dad painted it."

"He is really good!" Emma said sincerely.

"Thanks," Sam said. "Your hot chocolate is ready."

Moving over to the couch, Emma and Sam sat and drank their hot chocolate.

"Didn't you say that your parents are coming in for Thanksgiving?" Emma asked.

"Yes," Sam answered. "I am really looking forward to their visit."

"So, when are you going to start decorating?" Emma asked. "By the way, this is very good hot chocolate!"

"I told you that you would like it," Sam said with a smile. "Would you like more?"

When she shook her head no, Sam said, "I'm going to start decorating as soon as I finish my hot chocolate. Would you like to help out with that as well or do you have plans this afternoon?"

"I can help for a while," Emma answered.

"Great!" Sam said, obviously pleased she was staying. "When we are done with our hot chocolate, we'll head to the attic to bring down the decorations that I have, which isn't much."

"My mom has so many decorations that at times it has looked like the North Pole at their house," Emma said, laughing as she pictured how their yard and house would soon be transformed.

"Well, I'm looking forward to seeing that!" Sam laughed. "Maybe your Mom can give me some advice on what to buy and what goes where."

"I am sure she would love to," Emma told him. "She's out shopping now, but when she gets back we can ask her to come over and see what you already have."

"Great," Sam said, then smiled. "When my mother comes to visit, she likes to redo my decorating. She never criticizes and always says I did great, but when I'm not at home, she'll move things around. Then she'll ask me, 'Doesn't it look better, but if you don't then I'll put it back.' Honestly, my house always looks better after my mom is done with it."

"Do you help your mom decorate?" Sam asked her.

"No! That is her thing, and like you, I might put the wrong decoration in the wrong spot," Emma explained. "I stay out of her way and so does Dad."

"Are you looking forward to the holidays?" Sam asked her.

"Yes, it's my favorite time of the year," Emma said.

"I heard hesitation in your voice, are you sure it's your favorite time of year?" Sam asked.

"Yes, it's just my Dad," Emma started, wondering if she really wanted to share any more with Sam. "He writes these Christmas Letters every year. Starting today until Christmas my family doesn't really see him much."

Emma stood and went over to look at his fish, then continued, "He's always in his office writing."

"That's a bad thing?" Sam asked.

"Yes, when these letters take him away from his family," Emma tried to explain. "I know he really enjoys writing them, but as the years have gone by, especially last year, he seems to spend more time with strangers than he does with his family. That's where I have the problem. Christmas is supposed to be about family and I just can't get through to Dad that he should be spending more time with us, especially Mom. Dad says he is doing God's will, but I'm not so sure."

"What does your mom say, if you don't mind me asking?" Sam asked quietly.

"She says that I should respect his wishes and keep my mouth shut, so to speak," Emma said sadly.

"I hear what you are saying," Sam said, getting up and feeding his fish, "You said it yourself, though, your Dad is doing God's will."

"I said he thinks he is doing God's will, but is he?" Emma questioned.

"You don't think so?" Sam asked.

"I'm not sure," Emma shared. "I'm just wondering if my Dad is hearing correctly."

Shaking her head and looking at Sam sadly, Emma explained, "Look, I love that my Dad wants to do God's work, but a couple of years ago my Dad had a heart attack because he was doing way too much. He was still teaching English and writing his Christmas Letters. Sam, I was never so scared! We could have lost him!"

"But you didn't," Sam said softly.

"No, thank God, and last year Mom had to threaten to burn every envelope and letterhead we had if he didn't slow down. That was the only thing he responded to and now here we are again," Emma said as she sat back down on his couch.

"Now you are afraid he will overdo it again?" Sam asked.

"Yes," Emma said as tears rolled down her cheek.

Grabbing a box of Kleenex, Sam said, "Emma, I'm sorry."

Taking a deep breath, Emma pulled herself together and asked, "So where are those decorations you were talking about?"

"In the attic over the garage," Sam said jumping up to lead the way.

Emma and Sam made their way out to his garage, and while Sam was up in the attic Emma suddenly felt guilty.

"Sam, I don't mind my Dad writing his Christmas Letters, I just don't like that it takes so much of his time and it stresses him out," she explained. "Mom writes out Christmas cards with a letter about our family and it takes her about a week to get them all done and sent out."

"I get it, you want to spend more time with your Dad," Sam said. "I wish I could, too. My parents travel a lot since Dad retired so they are always on the go. That's why I am really looking forward to them being here for a while."

"Well, I am looking forward to meeting them," Emma said with a smile.

"You will," Sam said handing Emma another box from the attic. "I think that's it."

"There are only six boxes," Emma said with surprise thinking how many her mother had stashed in their attic.

"I know and most of these boxes are Christmas lights," Sam told her.

"So, where do you want to begin?" Emma asked.

Coming down the ladder Sam answered, "Christmas lights, you can start with untangling this knot."

"This might take me a while," Emma told him laughing, but the lights untangled easier than she was expecting.

As Sam got out his ladder and put it up along the gutter of his house, Emma finished untangling them and then handed him the lights, one string at a time. As they put up his Christmas lights, they continued to talk about Christmas, family, and found they had a lot in common.

Coming down the ladder, Sam said, "That should be it. Now let's hope they all go on."

Making his way to the power outlet, Sam hit the switch and every light lit up.

"They work!" Sam said excitedly. "Emma, I can't thank you enough."

"It was my pleasure," Emma said sincerely realizing she'd had a good time.

"I owe you big time," Sam told her, giving her a big hug.

"No, you don't," Emma said.

Emma's phone rang, answering, Emma said, "Hi, Mom. Thanks, I'll tell him."

"Mom says your lights look great, but to put them on a timer so they come on and off when you want them to." Emma told Sam.

"I don't know, Mom, hold on, I'll ask him."

"Mom wants to know if you would like to come to dinner," Emma asked him.

"Sure, thanks," Sam said enthusiastically.

"What time do you want us to come over, Mom?" Emma asked her Mom.

"Mom says whenever we are done here we can head over," Emma told him.

"Then we'll be done soon," Sam laughed.

"Love, you, too, Mom, bye."

After she hung up with her Mom, Emma turned to Sam, "I didn't mean to put you on the spot. If you have other plans, I understand."

"No, I don't," Sam laughed. "Emma, I have to say something about your Dad's writing, though, if I could. It seems to me that this is very important to him, so maybe you should support him and not fight him. In fact, maybe if you helped him then it would not take him so long to write them."

"My Dad doesn't want any help," Emma explained. "Mom and I used to ask every year and every year we received the same answer. Dad would say, 'This is my project and I have to do it.'"

Emma walked over to the power switch and turned off his lights and asked, "Do you have a timer we can use?"

"I do, but it's in the house. Don't go away, I'll be right back."

As Sam walked into his house, Emma felt ashamed. She knew Sam and her Mom were right which just made her feel that much worse. In her heart, she knew it, too. She waited until Sam returned, took the timer, set it up, and turned it on.

Then she looked straight up into Sam's eyes, "I appreciate your honesty and you are right. It is important to my Dad, so I will try to respect his decision."

"He will appreciate it," Sam said as they walked to her parents' home together.

"Hello, Mom, Dad we're here," Emma called out.

"Emma, Sam, you have been busy. I hope you are both hungry," Ruth said.

"I know I am," Sam said. "Thank you for inviting me."

"Me, too, Mom thanks for dinner," Emma smiled.

"Emma, go get your Dad and tell him the food is on the table," Ruth said.

"I'll get him," Sam offered. "Where is he?"

"He's in his office right down the hall," Ruth said as she pointed him in the right direction.

Sam walked down the hall to Frank's office and knocked, "Excuse me, Frank, Ruth says dinner is on the table."

"Hello, Sam," Frank said getting up from behind his desk and reaching his hand out. "It's good to see you, again"

"It's good to see you again, too, Frank. It looks like I interrupted you, though," Sam replied.

"You did, but that's quite alright," Frank said with a smile.

"Were you thinking about the letters you are going to write?" Sam asked.

"How do you know about the letters?" Frank said surprised. "Wait, let me guess, Emma."

"I suppose she told you that I spend more time in here writing to strangers than I do with my own family," Frank said.

"She mentioned that she wished she saw you more during over the holidays," Sam admitted.

"She refuses to accept what I am doing has special meaning," Frank said sadly.

"If it helps any, I told her that since it is so important to you, she should support your decision," Sam confessed.

"You told her that?" Frank walked around his desk and held out his hand again. "Thank you, Sam, that means a lot."

Both men walked into the kitchen and sat down to eat. With Frank and Ruth at the ends of the table, Emma sat directly across from Sam.

"Let's bow our heads to give thanks for this food," Frank said leading them in prayer.

During dinner, they all spoke what was coming head, Thanksgiving, Emma's Thanksgiving Pageant, and Christmas.

When dinner was over, Sam asked Frank to follow him back to his house, "I have something you might find interesting. In fact, you should all come over."

"I wonder what that is all about," Ruth said as she and Emma finished washing dishes from dinner.

"I don't know, but we'll find out soon enough," Emma said as curious as her Mom.

Walking over to Sam's house, and inspecting his lights, Ruth said, "Your house looks beautiful, Sam. You and Emma did a great job!"

"Thanks Ruth, Emma was a huge help."

Once they were in Sam's house, Emma's parents couldn't help but admire Sam's home, especially the fish tank.

"I always wanted one of these," Ruth said.

"It's very relaxing just watching the fish," Sam said with a smile.

"I would rather catch them then watch them," Frank laughed.

"Make yourself comfortable," Sam invited, "I'll be right back."

While Sam was gone, Emma showed her parents the picture that Sam's dad painted.

When Sam returned carrying a box, a box, Ruth said, "Sam, this painting is beautiful!"

"My Dad has painted for as long as I can remember," Sam told them. "That one is definitely my favorite, though."

"What do you have there?" Frank asked.

Handing Frank the long rectangular box, Sam told him, "Go ahead and open it."

When Frank opened the box there was an old-fashioned pen and ink bottle cartridge kit inside.

"Where did you get this?" Frank asked.

"It belonged to my grandfather," Sam told them.

"It's beautiful!" Ruth said as she came over and admired it.

"It is indeed beautiful," Frank said handing it back to Sam.

Shaking his head, Sam said, "Frank, I want you to have it."

"I can't accept this," Frank said trying again to hand the box back to Sam.

"Frank, it has been sitting in my drawer for almost a year collecting dust," Sam told him. "I was thinking you could use the pen for your letters."

"Are you sure you want to part with it?" Frank asked. "Isn't it an antique?"

"It is and I'm sure I want you to have it," Sam said firmly.

"Then I shall use it with pride, Sam," Frank said reaching out to shake Sam's hand. "Thank you very much."

Emma sat on the couch and said nothing, she knew for sure her dad would never stop writing his Christmas letters.

"Emma, you're quiet, what do you think?" her Dad asked her.

Getting up and looking at the antique pen, she said politely, "I think it is very nice of Sam to think of you, but I think it should stay in his family."

"Emma," Sam said firmly. "If I keep it it's going to continue to collect dust and I know my grandfather would want someone to use it and love it as much as he did. A set like this should be used and I have no use for an antique pen."

Turning to her Dad, Sam said, "Frank, the pen is yours."

"Thanks again, Sam," Frank said. "I promise I will take good care of it."

"I'm sure you will," Sam said with a smile.

"Well, I think it's time we head back home," Frank said turning toward the door.

"Emma, can I talk to you for a minute before you go?" Sam asked.

After Frank and Ruth left, Sam said, "Emma, you don't approve of me giving the pen to your Dad, do you?"

"It was very sweet of you," Emma said sincerely. "It's just that now I know he will never stop writing."

"Did you see the look on your Dad's face?" Sam pointed out. "He was happy. He looked like a child on Christmas morning."

"I have to admit I have never seen my Dad that happy," Emma admitted with a smile.

"That should tell you something," Sam said to her.

"It does," Emma agreed. "Mom seemed pleased with it, too, which doesn't make sense, because he won't be spending time with her either."

"I guess your mom is use to it," Sam said.

"She has told me that she misses him, but still she says nothing. There is definitely more to this and I am going to find out what it is," Emma said with resolve. "I really need to go, Sam. It was fun today, thanks. I will see you Monday morning. Good night, Sam."

"Good night, Emma, thanks again for all of your help today."

Emma moved her car back to her parents' home and went right into her Dad's office.

"Can I see it?" she asked.

"Sure," Frank said handing it to her. "What do you think?"

"It is indeed beautiful. I have never seen a pen like this before," Emma told her Dad.

"Me neither," her Dad said. "However, I sense a 'but,' though."

"I suppose you'll be writing more now that you have this special pen," Emma stated.

"No, I won't," he said firmly. "It doesn't work that way, Emma. I am still planning on writing the same number of letters."

Getting up from his chair, her Dad came around the desk and gave her a hug, "It's getting late, see you at church in the morning."

Emma told her parents good night and drove home listening to the soft instrumental Christmas music she had in her phone. Picturing her Dad's face light up when he opened that antique pen box put a smile on Emma's face. Once she was home, Emma had a hard time falling asleep. She couldn't stop thinking about her parents, Sam, and that antique pen.

Chapter 3

Sunday morning, Emma woke up to her phone going off. "What are you doing this afternoon?" it read from Sam.

Emma texted back, "I'm going out to lunch with my parents. Why?"

"Can you help me decorate the inside of my house?" Sam asked.

"Sure, what time?" Emma asked.

"Three okay?" asked Sam.

"Three it is," Emma texted back.

She laid her phone down and smiled as she drifted back to sleep.

What felt like just a few minutes later, Emma looked over at her clock and realized it was later than she thought. If she didn't hurry, she would be late for church. Running out of the house and jumping into her car, she cranked up the music and headed to church. Once she was there, she walked swiftly up the steps trying not to fall in her brand new high-heel shoes. She looked around and spotted her parents in their usual spot.

As she listened to the sermon and the music, she couldn't help but look around to see if she could spot Sam.

Leaning over, her Mom asked, "Who are you looking for?"

"Sam," Emma whispered. "He told me he was going to be here, but I don't see him. I'm sure he's here somewhere."

Smiling, her mother said, "I'm sure he is, too."

When the sermon was over, Emma told her parents, "I need to speak to Jennifer. I'll be right out so we can go to lunch."

Emma made her way to the front of the church where Jennifer was speaking to their pastor.

"Good morning, Emma!" said the pastor with a smile.

"Good morning, Pastor Phil!" Emma responded.

"Running a little late this morning, were you?" he asked with a smile.

Emma looked puzzled, "Yes, Pastor Phil. I will admit I almost overslept, but I am so glad I didn't. Today's message really hit home for me."

"I'm glad to hear it," Pastor Phil said. "Jennifer, Emma, have a great day."

"Bye, Pastor Phil," they responded in unison.

"How did he know I overslept?" Emma asked Jennifer shaking her head.

"You have to remember that when you come in late, he notices," Jennifer laughed.

"I'll have to remember that," Emma said.

"I don't think you'll have to worry too much about that," Jennifer smiled. "You are always on time."

"What's going on?" Jennifer asked realizing Emma had sought her out.

"I need to talk to you, but I can't right now. I'm going to lunch with mom and dad and then I am helping Sam decorate the inside of his house," Emma explained.

"That sounds like fun," Jennifer said. "You're right, though, we do need to talk. Give me a call when you get home."

The two girls hugged, and Emma made her way outside to her parents' car. Sam was standing there speaking to them.

"Phil noticed that you were late didn't he?" her Dad commented.

"Yes, and I told him that I am so glad I didn't oversleep. What a great message!" Emma answered.

"I agree," Ruth said, then turned to Sam. "Sam would you like to join us for lunch?"

"Not today, thanks. I need to shop for more Christmas decorations," Sam answered. "Emma has promised to help me this afternoon, so I need to get a move on."

Turning to Emma, Sam said, "Emma, I'll see you at three then?"

"Yes, you will," Emma said as she watched Sam walk to his truck.

I hope lunch goes by quickly, she thought to herself, looking forward to her afternoon with Sam knowing this will be the last time she would be hanging out with Sam.

After lunch, Emma ran home and changed into her favorite jeans and hoodie and made her way to Sam's. Cranking up the music, she sang the whole way there. When she reached his house, she saw her Dad outside raking. She waved to him as she ran up to Sam's front door. Knocking on his front door, Emma waited. When there was no answer, she looked at her watch and saw she was right on time. Knocking again she thought, *"Where is he? His truck is in the driveway, so I know he's back from shopping.*

"Hello," she called out.

No answer, but she heard a loud thump from back near the garage.

Walking over to his garage, she yelled again, "Hello?"

"Just a minute, Emma," came a muffled voice from inside the garage.

I wonder what he is doing? she thought.

Opening up his garage, he smiled warmly at Emma.

"What are you doing in there?" Emma asked.

"Getting my decorations out," Sam replied.

"I thought we did that yesterday," Emma said.

"We did but I wanted to see what else we needed before I went shopping," Sam said with an excited smile. "Wait until you see what I bought!"

"Where do you want to begin?" Emma asked looking at the pile of boxes.

"We need to get these boxes into the house," Sam explained.

Picking up box closest to her feet, she said, "Okay, I'll start with this one."

"I think you can handle one more," Sam said as he grabbed another box and laid it on top of the first box.

"Great, now I can barely see," Emma complained. "How did you know this box wouldn't be too heavy?"

"That's easy, I know what's in these boxes," Sam laughed. "Careful, now. Don't fall."

When Emma carefully put her boxes down on the floor inside the house, she could not believe her eyes. It looked as if Sam had bought out the entire Christmas department.

"Wow!" she exclaimed, as she noticed the three-foot angel sitting in the corner. "Now do you think you have enough decorations?"

"Probably, but you never know with my mom," Sam laughed. "You see my mom loves Christmas and in her mind, you can never have enough decorations."

"My mom does the same thing," Emma said shaking her head. "She has given me way too many decorations for my place, too."

Emma and Sam opened boxes and began placing decorations around the room. Emma put an angel on a shelf, a ceramic ginger bread house on the end table, and a Christmas pillow on the sofa. Sam placed a huge Santa near the fireplace, then hung up three stockings, strung lights around the mantle, and hung a huge Christmas Wreath above the fireplace. Emma carefully arranged a nativity scene on the coffee table.

Sam's house was ready for the holidays. They finished up by working together to wrap greenery down the bannister. It didn't take them long to turn his living room into a beautiful Christmas wonderland.

As they sat on the sofa admiring their success, Sam asked, "How about a cup of hot chocolate?"

"Yes, that would be great," Emma answered remembering his great recipe for the traditional winter treat.

"Coming right up," Sam assured her as he headed into his kitchen.

As Emma sat on his sofa looking around at all they had accomplished, she asked, "Are you putting up a tree?"

"Yes, but I was hoping to find a place where I could buy a real tree," Sam answered from the kitchen.

"There is a place on the edge of town called Hank's Tree Farm," Emma told him.

"Great," Sam said. "I'm planning on getting one Thanksgiving weekend when my parents are here."

Sam made his way into the living room with two cups of hot chocolate.

"There you go," Sam said as he handed Emma a Christmas mug of steaming hot chocolate. "Be careful it's very hot."

"Wow! You even added marshmallows," she commented as she wrapped her hands around the beautiful mug.

"I hope you like marshmallows," Sam said, thinking maybe he should have asked her first.

"I do, just not a lot," Emma answered with a smile.

"I'm glad I guessed right," Sam said as he sat down beside her.

"You did great, thank you," Emma assured him as she sipped her hot chocolate. "You know, I should be mad at you for giving that antique pen set to my Dad, but I can't deny how happy it made him, so thank you."

"What was I going to do with it?" Sam said, relieved she wasn't angry with him. "Besides now it will be used by someone who truly appreciates such things. I know how much you miss your Dad when he's writing, but supporting him by not giving him a hard time will make him even happier than that pen set."

"Oh, I don't know about that, but I will support him," Emma answered quietly. "I think the reason I have such a hard time with it is that Dad was always around when I was little. Now that I'm older, I want to spend as much time as I can with him and Mom, especially after his illness."

"That is understandable," Sam agreed, "but you have to remember to live your own life and let them live theirs, too."

Suddenly getting up from the sofa, Sam said, "I almost forgot, would you like a cookie to go with your hot chocolate?"

"You baked?" Emma asked. "I didn't know you could bake!"

"Yeah, I couldn't sleep last night so I threw a batch of cookies in the oven," Sam explained. "Mom told me to get to a woman's heart is to know how to cook and especially bake."

"Is that what you are doing?" Emma asked turning to look him in the eyes. "Are you trying to get to my heart?"

"Maybe," Sam smiled as he leaned over and kissed Emma softly.

Surprised at his spontaneous act, he leaned back and said, "Should I not have done that?"

"This is not a good idea," Emma said shaking her head.

"Why?" Sam asked.

"Because you're the Assistant Principal and I am a teacher," Emma answered. "It wouldn't look right and I know that Jennifer would not approve. I think I'd better go."

"Emma, I'm sorry, I didn't think," Sam said shaking his head.

"I know, me neither," Emma said standing up.

Quickly grabbing her coat, Emma said, "See you tomorrow morning, Sam."

"Thanks for your help," Sam called out as she raced out the door.

Emma got in her car, turned up the heat and the radio, and drove home, but this time she did not sing.

What was I thinking? she said to herself. *Girl you better get a grip. I can only imagine what Jennifer is going to say. I'm sure she has a long speech already planned out and I am never going to hear the end of this.*

When Emma got home, she called Jennifer and immediately told her all about her Dad's new pen, then asked, "So, what do you think, Jenn?"

"I think you should let your Dad be your Dad and you should respect his decision which is what we have all been saying but you have been ignoring," Jenn answered her.

Here it comes, Emma thought. She could tell by Jennifer's tone she meant business.

"I'm glad you called, Emma," Jennifer said in a serious tone. "We need to talk about something else."

"Before you say anything," Emma interrupted her, holding back her tears, "I know what you are going to say and all I can say is you don't have to worry about me. I am not about to cross the line."

Emma waited, but Jennifer was silent, "Jenn, are you there?"

"I am, Emma," she said in softer tone. "What happened?"

Her friend knew her well, so between sobs Emma told Jennifer about the wonderful weekend she'd had with Sam. Then she shared how when he kissed her tonight she felt something that she had not felt in a very long time, but had told him they couldn't pursue it because he was the Assistant Principal and she was a teacher.

"Emma, I'm sorry," Jenn said gently, realizing how hard that was for Emma.

"Jenn, he's wonderful and we have a connection and it's not fair," Emma said trying hard to gather her emotions. "I think God is punishing me for trying to stop Dad from writing his Christmas Letters."

"Emma, that's not true and you know it," Jennifer said firmly.

"Do I?" asked Emma almost angrily.

"Emma," Jenn asked, "Do you trust God? Do you have faith in Him?"

"Yes," Emma answered quietly.

"Then rely on that and you'll be fine," her friend said kindly.

Jennifer always made Emma feel better.

Wiping her eyes, she changed the subject and asked, "How did your meeting go on Friday?"

"Well, it was rather long, but we got things resolved," Jenn answered, wisely letting the subject of Emma's relationship with Sam drop.

"Great! See you tomorrow then," Emma said.

"No, actually you won't," Jenn told her. "I have meetings off campus all day. If there are any issues, let Sam know. He's in charge."

"Does he know that?" Emma asked, surprised Sam hadn't mentioned it.

"No, I thought I would let him see the note I left on his desk Friday after everyone left," she said as both women laughed.

Chapter 4

Early the next morning, Emma woke up before her alarm went off. With her coffee in hand, she sat in her window seat and thought about her day. *Would she see Sam? How was she supposed to act around him? Could she really keep her emotions in check?*

When she got to school, she saw the light on in the nurse's office and went in to speak to her mom.

"Good morning, Mom, you're here early," she said with a smile.

"So are you," Ruth said greeting her daughter. "Is everything alright?"

"Everything is fine," Emma knew school was not the place to talk to her mom about Sam or her dad. "I'll see you at lunch."

Walking into her classroom, Emma looked at her students. She shook her head as it was obvious they did not want to be there including Emma. In fact, most of them were half asleep. Emma took a deep breath and thought, *four weeks until Thanksgiving and eight weeks until Christmas I can do this.*

The morning started out slow. It seemed no one wanted to come back to school after their fun Halloween weekend, but Emma made the best of it. By lunch her students were smiling and Emma realized they actually accomplished quite a bit after all. At lunch, she told her mom what her class did that morning and how Sam's house looked after they put up all the decorations.

"You never help me out decorating," Ruth said with a knowing smile.

"That's because the last time I tried to help, you rearranged all of the decorations I laid out," Emma answered.

"No, I didn't," Ruth said trying not to laugh.

"Yes, you did," Emma accused her teasingly, "Just ask Dad."

"Well, I have specific places for certain decorations," her Mom explained.

"Sam's mom sounds a lot like you, Mom," Emma smiled. "He said his mom loves Christmas as much as you do and that all of the decorations have to be perfect."

"She sounds like a very smart woman," Ruth laughed.

"No doubt," Emma smiled.

"By the way, can I get a ride to school with you tomorrow?" Ruth asked.

"Of course, I'll see you in the morning then, Mom," Emma answered as she got up and made her way back to her classroom.

The afternoon went by quickly and Emma wasted no time in gathering her stuff and making her way to the front door.

Spotting Josh on the front steps, she asked him, "Did you miss the bus?"

"No, my mom is picking me up," Josh told her. "She has a doctor's appointment."

"Oh, is she sick?" Emma asked, concerned about his mom and the baby.

"No, but guess what!" Josh said very excitedly.

"What?" Emma asked wondering what was going on.

"Today, I get to listen to my baby brother's heartbeat," Josh said with a huge smile on his face.

"WOW! That sounds exciting!" Emma said sharing his excitement.

Seeing Josh's mom pull up, Emma walked him down to their car.

"Hi, Stacey, Josh was just telling me that today he gets to listen to his baby brother's heartbeat," Emma said with a smile as she opened the door for Josh to get in the car.

"That's right, he has been pestering me about it, so I called the doctor to see if it was alright and she said it wasn't a problem," Stacey explained with a smile.

"Come on, Mom, let's go," Josh said impatiently.

"You two better get going," Emma smiled. "Josh, I want to hear all about it tomorrow, okay?"

Josh nodded as he and his mom headed out for their adventure.

Emma smiled as she made her way to her car. She turned her music up and sang all the way home. After she made herself dinner, she sat in her window seat thinking about the beautiful pen Sam gave to her Dad, her Mom, and the Thanksgiving pageant her class would put on the Friday before Thanksgiving. With all that she had on her plate, she prayed that God would give her the wisdom she needed to get through the next couple of weeks.

The next morning, Emma jumped out of bed realizing she almost forgot she was picking up her mom for school. Finding an outfit today seemed to take a lot of time for Emma. Running out the door and jumping into her car, she turned up the music and headed toward her parents' home. Honking her horn, Emma waited impatiently.

"Come on, Mom, we're going to be late," she said out loud as she honked again.

Just as she was about to get out of her car, her mom came walking out the front door.

"Why didn't you come in and say hello to your dad this morning?" her mom asked as she got in the car.

"I don't want to be late," Emma said impatiently.

"We're never late, and besides we're only ten minutes from school," Ruth said wondering why her daughter was so agitated. "What's going on?"

"Nothing, I just didn't want to hit traffic," Emma said as she backed out of her parents' driveway.

"What traffic and why are you dressed up today?" her mom asked.

"No reason," Emma answered. "I just wanted to, that's all."

Emma could never fool her mom. Ruth knew the reason it took her so long to pick out a striking outfit. Ruth and Emma made it to school in no time. Immediately, Emma noticed Sam's truck was in his parking space.

"Sam's here already," Emma said.

"I could have told you that," Ruth said. "He left about thirty minutes ago."

"You were watching him?" Emma asked looking at her mother with surprise.

"No, I just happen to look out my window this morning as he was leaving," Ruth responded getting out of the car.

They walked into school which was still quiet, gave each other a quick hug, and each went their own way. When Emma reached her classroom, she turned on the light, opened the blinds, took off her coat, and prepared her day.

"Miss Emma," a voice called out, but Emma was so focused she hadn't noticed Josh standing in front of her desk.

"Miss Emma," he yelled startling Emma. "Are you alright?"

"I'm fine, how are you Josh?" Emma asked looking up at her favorite student.

"I'm okay," he said handing Emma a sonogram picture of his brother. "Here look!"

"WOW! Look at him! Josh, it's amazing!" Emma said with a big smile. "It looks like he's sucking his thumb. What a gift God has given your family."

"Can you walk me down to see Ms. Ruth?" Josh asked her. "I want to show her the picture, too."

"I think you can do it yourself, can't you?" Emma suggested. "Just don't be gone long."

"Sure, I'll be right back," Josh said excitedly and ran out of the classroom down to the nurse's station.

"Why are you all dressed up, Miss Emma?" Sally asked as she walked into the classroom.

Sally was one of her students who noticed everything.

"It's a new dress, what do you think? I was thinking about wearing it at the Thanksgiving Pageant," Emma twirled.

"I like it. It matches your eyes." Sally smiled.

If Sally noticed, I'm sure everybody else is going to as well, including Sam, Emma thought. *I should have never changed my clothes this morning, wearing an emerald velvet dress to school, now it looks like I am trying to impress the new Assistant Principal. Real smart, Emma!*

"Josh, good morning! What can I do for you?" Ruth asked as she slid her chair over to him. "Do you have a stomach ache again this morning?"

"Nope," he answered pulling out the picture of his baby brother. "I have something to show you. See, Miss Ruth it's my baby brother."

"Josh, he looks just like you," Ruth said with a smile.

Staring at the picture, Josh asked, "How can you tell?"

Ruth smiled, "I'm kidding, but I am sure when he arrives, he will look just like you did when you were born."

"Do you really think so?" Josh asked.

"I do," Ruth said, then asked him, "Now did you eat breakfast this morning?"

"Yes," he smiled, beaming from the thought his baby brother might look like him.

"Thank you for showing me his picture," Ruth smiled. "How's your mom today?"

"She threw up this morning," Josh said shaking his head. "I think I better stay here a while in case I get sick, too."

"If you stay, I'm going to have to call your dad," Ruth told him trying not to smile.

"My Dad!" Josh sprung up from the bed. "Why not my mom?"

"Well, if your Mom is sick, I don't want her to make all of the rest of the children sick," Ruth explained. "Besides, your Dad told me last week if you come down anymore, I need to call him."

"I'm feeling a lot better, Miss Ruth," Josh said as he quickly headed back to class.

When Emma saw Josh coming down the hallway, she lined up her students for music class.

"Does anyone smell fresh cookies?" she asked her students.

"Yes!" Sally answered, sniffing the air. "Makes me hungry!"

After Emma dropped off her students, Emma spotted Jennifer coming out of her office eating a cookie.

"Where did you get that?" Emma asked.

"Sam brought them in, help yourself, they are on the conference table," Jennifer answered. "We are still invited to your parents' home for Thanksgiving, right?"

"Yes," Emma confirmed.

"Great! That was so nice of your mom to invite us," Jennifer said. "Send me a text of what you want me to bring."

"I'll have Mom do that," Emma promised.

"How are you?" Jennifer asked.

"I'm fine, but we do need to talk," Emma smiled.

"Yes, we do," Jennifer agreed as she gave her friend a quick hug. "I'll call you later."

As Jennifer made her way to her office, she saw two boys in the hall, "Why aren't you boys in class?"

"We had to use the restroom, Miss Jennifer," one of the boys answered respectfully.

"Didn't you hear the bell?" she asked. "Quickly, get to class and remember, I'm watching you."

Emma poked her head into the conference room. Spotting the cookies, Emma grabbed one and took a bite. *These are so good she,* told herself.

"I'm glad you like them," said a voice from behind her.

"Sam," Emma exclaimed, "Did you bake these?"

"Sure did," Sam answered nodding his head. "Sorry, I didn't mean to startle you."

"You couldn't sleep so you baked?" Emma guessed.

"Yes, but this time, I baked for the entire staff," Sam said.

"That's a lot of cookies," Emma said. "As a teacher, I thank you!"

"Your welcome," Sam said, then asked. "Do you have a minute?"

"I have a few minutes," Emma answered. "My kids are at music."

As they sat in the conference room, Emma asked, "What made you pick a field in education?"

"My Mom and Dad are both former teachers," Sam answered. "My mom taught high school Science for twenty years and my Dad was a Physical Education teacher and a baseball coach for a number of years. Plus, I enjoy having the summers off!"

"I'd rather be walking the halls and checking on the kids then being stuck in a classroom. Being an Assistant Principal allows me to meet all of the students and interact with them and their parents," Sam shared. "I spend very little time in my office. I would much rather be checking on the students and helping teachers wherever it is needed."

"I can tell you Jennifer will definitely keep you busy," Emma told him. "It is a good thing you came along when you did. She has been overwhelmed since Beth went on maternity leave. Jennifer would much rather be in her office handling other matters than running around the school."

"Well, I am thrilled to be here," Sam said sincerely. "So, have you known Jennifer long?"

"Yes," Emma smiled. "We went to college together and we're best friends, which means we tell each other everything."

"I will definitely keep that in mind," Sam said, remembering what had happened yesterday.

"Well, it's time for me to go back to class," Emma said as she took two more cookies. "One for Mom and one for me for after lunch."

Sam stood up and asked, "Can we do dinner tonight? I would like to apology for the mistake I made yesterday. I promise I will be on my best behavior."

"Dinner will be fine then," Emma grinned.

"What time should I pick you up?" Sam asked.

"I'll meet you at seven at the diner," Emma answered thinking that would be more acceptable behavior.

"Seven it is," Sam said, glad she had agreed to dinner.

After school, Emma drove her Mom home thinking about what she was going to say to her Dad. Ruth invited her to stay for dinner, but Emma told her she was meeting Sam at the diner. She said she wanted to come in and see her Dad for a few minutes, though.

Walking down the hall into her Dad's office, Emma took a deep breath before she knocked on his door.

"Dad, I want to talk to you a minute," Emma said as she hugged her dad. "I just wanted you to know that I am going to try to support your writing. I know how much these letters mean to you, so if writing them makes you happy, then I'm on board with it."

Stunned, Frank looked at her and said nothing at first.

Then smiling broadly, he said, "You have no idea how much this means to me, Emma."

Hugging his daughter, he added emotionally, "Emma, I love you."

"I love you, too, Dad," Emma said as she returned his hug. "Now, I need to freshen up before I go meet Sam for dinner."

Emma winked and smiled at her Mom as she headed out for the diner.

When Emma reached the diner, Sam wasn't there yet so Emma decided that now would be a good time to text Jennifer and let her know that she was having dinner with Sam and that she was going to ask him to help her with the Thanksgiving pageant.

It didn't take Jennifer long to text back, "That's a great idea and thank you for telling me. Emma, I trust you."

Emma smiled as she read the text since she had not been sure what her friend was going to say.

"Who are you texting" Sam asked as he walked up and slid in the booth across from her.

"Jennifer," Emma told him and she smiled at him in greeting.

"Is having dinner together okay?" Sam asked her.

"We're fine," Emma told him shaking her head. "I was just asking Jenn if I could use you."

"Use me?" Sam asked cautiously.

"Yes, with the Thanksgiving pageant," Emma explained.

"I was going to ask you about this Thanksgiving pageant I keep hearing about," Sam said.

"Let's order first then I'll tell you all about it," Emma suggested.

"The pageant is really cute," Emma explained, taking a drink of her sweet tea. "My students are going to tell a story they wrote themselves on how they think Thanksgiving got started."

"Well, that sounds interesting," Sam laughed.

"Interesting to say the least," Emma agreed, laughing. "It amazes me what these kids come up with. I can't wait for you to see it."

"Me neither," Sam said with a smile. "So, what can I do to help?"

"I'm glad you asked," Emma smiled.

"Wait a minute," Sam stopped Emma, "This is what you were talking about when you said you asked Jennifer if you could use me?"

"Yep," Emma laughed.

"I will be glad to help out," Sam smiled. "Do you think your Dad will make the pageant?"

"Of course, Dad has never missed one yet," Emma answered, surprised at his question. "Why do you ask?"

"I know how busy he is this time of year with his writing," Sam said, suddenly wishing he had not brought up the subject.

"Yes, he is but he always takes time out to come to see the pageant," Emma explained. "Dad knows how important it is to me. The kids work hard, and I want my parents to see what my kids have come up with."

I hope she's right and Frank does come, Sam thought to himself.

Sam wisely changed the subject and they enjoyed the rest of their evening.

Emma was glad she came and did not want their evening to end. Keeping their relationship low key was definitely going to be a challenge.

Chapter 5

Thanksgiving was three weeks away and Emma couldn't wait. The Thanksgiving pageant was the Friday night the week before Thanksgiving and Emma had a lot to do before then. Every day she stayed after school either having a meeting or a rehearsal. Even though Emma was overwhelmed, she couldn't be happier.

Day after day, Emma prepared her class for the upcoming pageant. The kids were learning their lines. Between costumes, props, the set, and lighting, Emma's days were long and tiring, but she knew this year's pageant would be the best one yet. She could not wait until her parents saw it, especially her Dad since she had not seen much of him with his writing schedule and with her pageant preparations. The kids were ready. She was exhausted, the work involved was enormous, but she loved coordinating the pageant and being busy kept her mind from her wandering to Sam and what could have been.

The day of the pageant finally arrived and as Emma put herself together that morning, she almost forgot that she was picking up her mom again. Running to her car, Emma turned up the music and glanced at herself in the mirror. After today she thought, *I can start thinking of the holidays. Next week is Thanksgiving and the start of the Christmas season.*

Emma could not be happier as she headed to her parents' home. Honking her horn, Emma waited rather impatiently.

Come on Mom, she said to herself. Honking again and about to run up to the front door, her mom appeared.

"Why didn't you come in?" her mom asked.

"Any other day I would, but not today," Emma said rather impatiently. "I have a million things to do today. I am just praying nothing goes wrong before the pageant tonight."

Ruth looked over to her daughter, "Well, you look beautiful!"

"I do?" Emma asked.

"Emma, are you alright? You seem more nervous," her mom said.

"Mom, it's the pageant," Emma responded.

Ruth stared at her daughter, "No, I don't think so, it's not the pageant. I have seen many pageants and you have never dressed this nice before. I think it has to do with an Assistant Principal."

"That's absurd!" Emma said. "I always dress nice for the pageant."

"Yes, but not this nice," Ruth replied knowingly. "Anyway, I am very proud of you."

"Thanks, Mom. That means a lot," Emma said sincerely. "I think this year's pageant is going to be the best you and Dad have ever seen. I can tell you that the kids have worked very hard on this pageant and they are so excited."

"Well, I can't wait to see it tonight," Ruth said enthusiastically.

"You mean you and Dad, right?" Emma asked, sensing something was wrong.

"I was hoping we could have this conversation later," Ruth said quietly.

"What?" Emma asked. "He's not coming? What? Why? Is he sick?"

"No, he is fine. He has one letter that must get out tomorrow," Ruth said. "Emma, he feels terrible, but this is important. We hope you understand."

Emma, could not believe what she was hearing. Her Dad, who promised her that he would be there and had never missed a pageant before, was not coming because of a letter. Fury rose up into Emma as she parked her car in the school parking lot.

Getting out of the car Emma turned and saw Sam. He had a look of fear on his face.

"What's wrong?" Emma asked.

"It's Josh," Sam answered. "Ruth, he's down at the nurse's station."

"Already?" Ruth said as she made her way into school quickly.

"That boy," Emma said, irritated. "I do not need this today."

"Emma, what's wrong?" Sam asked.

"I have a pageant to put on tonight, remember?" she answered impatiently.

"No," Sam said shaking his head. "I don't think that is it."

"Let's go deal with Josh," Emma said as she headed for the nurse's station.

When they reached her mom's office, Josh was already sitting on the examination table.

"I have a stomach ache, Mr. Sam," Josh said holding his stomach. "My mom threw up this morning."

"And now you think you have it?" Sam asked the boy.

"How did you know, Mr. Sam?" Josh asked.

Knowing the whole story of why Josh's mom was throwing up, Sam said, "Josh, I am sorry to hear you are not feeling well. I am also sorry I am going to have to send you home."

"Really?" Josh said excitedly.

"Yes," Sam said, "but that also means you will not be in the pageant tonight."

"Oh, I am sure I will feel better by tonight," Josh told Sam.

"I don't think so," Sam told him firmly. "Even if you are, you will not be allowed to participate in the pageant."

"You mean if I go home, I can't be in the pageant?" Josh asked with a look of shock on his face.

"That is exactly what I mean," Sam told him, sternly.

Josh hesitated and asked, "Miss Ruth, is he, right?"

"Yes," Ruth nodded.

"Miss Emma," Sam said. "We need to call Josh's Dad; do you have his number?"

"I do, but's it's back in my classroom," as tears started to run down her cheeks.

"Emma, it'll be okay," Sam said not knowing what to do.

Emma couldn't help it, the tears would not stop, "We are sure going to miss you tonight Josh. Now, I will have to find another pilgrim to take your place."

"Don't be sad, Miss Emma," Josh said, shocked to see his teacher crying.

"I can't help it Josh," Emma told him. "You are our best pilgrim and now, well, who knows how good the play will be. You see, Josh, what you do just doesn't affect you. Sure, you can go home and get well, but a lot of people are counting on you and will be disappointed."

As Emma tried to wipe away her tears, Ruth tried to console her daughter knowing the real reason behind those tears.

"I'll go get the number," Emma said sadly, turning to go to her classroom.

"I have it," Ruth said handing Sam a piece of paper.

As soon as Josh saw Sam dialing he jumped off the table, "Wait, I think it must have been something I ate this morning. I am feeling a little better, but I still have a stomach ache."

Kneeling down to Josh's level so he could look him right in the eye, Sam asked, "Do you feel like you have a butterfly in your stomach?"

"No, but it does feel tight," Josh said.

"Josh, I think what you have is a nervous stomach," Sam told the boy. "Are you nervous about tonight?"

Josh lowered his head and nodded, Sam smiled at Josh,

"It's okay, Josh. We all get nervous at times, but you are going to do just fine tonight."

"You think so?" Josh asked.

"I do!" Sam said.

"Then I better get to class," Josh smiled and headed for the door.

"Not so fast," Sam said. "Why does it seem like you can't stay in your classroom all day without coming to see Miss Ruth?"

"Because I like Miss Ruth," Josh said with a big smile.

They all smiled, and Emma wiped the last of her tears from her eyes.

"That's great Josh," Sam agreed. "We like her, too, but what if you didn't come down at all during the day and stopped by her office after school to get a gift?"

"What kind of gift?" Josh asked.

"Well, that depends on the day," Sam laughed. "But I can tell you that it is definitely worth the wait."

Josh looked up at Miss Ruth, "What kind of gift?"

"Smart," Sam whispered to Emma.

"One of the smartest in my class," Emma whispered back to Sam.

"Well, I don't know yet because you have never gone a day without coming to see me," Ruth told him. "I will think of something."

"Can you think of something by tomorrow?" Josh asked her.

"Oh, yes," Ruth said with a smile. "I can definitely come up with something by tomorrow."

"Then I will see you tomorrow after school," said Josh as he ran out the door and down to his classroom.

"I did not see that coming," Sam said, laughing.

"Me neither, but thanks to you both, I need to come up with a prize for that boy by tomorrow," Ruth laughed.

"Now you didn't think I would leave you hanging with this, did you?" Sam asked with a mysterious smile.

"What do you have in mind?" Emma asked.

"I don't know yet, but I am going to call Josh's mom and get some information," Sam told them. "I will see both of you tonight."

"Emma, are you alright?" her mom asked after Sam left, hugging her daughter. "I know you're disappointed and that is why your dad wants to take you out to lunch today so he can explain."

"Mom, I can't go today, I'm just too busy, but you go," Emma replied.

"Emma," her mom started.

"It's okay, Mom. I am not mad, just disappointed," Emma said. "Now I really have to get to class. We still have a lot to do to get ready for tonight."

Walking to her classroom, Emma tried to keep it together not only for herself, but for her kids. It was not her students' fault that her dad chose not to come this evening, so Emma put a smile on her face and entered her classroom.

"Good morning!" Emma said as she noticed most of her class was already there and conversing together. "I need everyone to sit down."

One of the little girls in her classroom came up to her, "Miss Emma, if we don't go see Miss Ruth all day, do we get a prize, too?"

Without thinking, Emma answered, "Sure, you all get a prize if you don't go down to the nurse's station, but if you are really sick, please go and you still might get a prize."

"So, we get a prize if we go or we don't go," Josh asked smiling.

"No, that's not how it works," Emma answered realizing this was getting confusing. "If you truly don't feel well, please go see Miss Ruth."

"Well, how do we know if we are really sick?" another child asked.

"Miss Ruth is very smart and she'll know," Emma shook her head, realizing this conversation was getting out of hand. "Now, before we start our day, I want you all to take a deep breath and close your eyes."

With her student's eyes shut, Emma herself took a breath, "Okay, now let's get this party started."

"Party on!" her students said.

"Yes, we are going to have an exciting day," Emma smiled at them. "I want all of you to relax. Tonight, is going to be a lot of fun. We've all worked very hard preparing for this pageant. So, we are going to have some quiet time during the day. I want you all to go get a book and read in small groups."

"Can we go over our lines?" Josh asked, glad he was going to be able to be the Pilgrim after all.

"Yes, if you do them quietly," Emma said as she went over to her desk trying to keep her composure and focus on tonight's pageant.

As the morning went on, Emma got a message from Jennifer asking her to meet her in her office for lunch.

"Are you alright?" Jennifer asked as she and Emma had lunch. "I know you have a lot to do for the pageant tonight."

"I'm fine, really, but I do want to talk about what you and your family want for Christmas and when are we going shopping?" Emma asked, carefully changing the subject.

Jennifer laughed as she handed Emma a piece of red paper, "It so happens I have a list for you from my boys. As for me, sometime with my husband would be nice. I can't tell you the last time we went out on a date, so whenever you're available, give me a call."

"I'll keep that in mind," Emma smiled. "Jenn, thank you so much."

"For what?" Jennifer asked.

"For being an amazing friend," Emma told her. "I am truly grateful for your friendship."

"Right back at you," Jenn smiled, holding up her glass to toast her friend.

After school, Emma made her way down to see her mom. She found her coming out of the restroom with a mask and gloves on.

"What happened or do I not want to know?" Emma asked her.

"You know Billy Garcia, fifth grade, polite, tall boy, right?" Ruth asked, taking off her mask.

"Yes, I know Billy, I think he's grown two inches since last year," Emma answered.

"Well, his grandmother is visiting and she made her famous chili," Ruth said.

"I love her chili," Emma said.

"Me, too," Ruth smiled. "Where do you think I got our recipe?"

"No wonder yours is the best around," Emma told her smiling.

"Thank you, dear," Ruth said taking off her gloves. "Billy tried to eat more than his older brother last night, though."

"His brother Bobby who is in high school?" Emma asked.

"Yes," her mom said shaking her head.

"Say no more," Emma said laughing. "Sorry, Mom, do you need any help?"

"No, but I imagine you are going to need some help getting ready for tonight," Ruth said. "I'll meet you in the gym later to help you."

"Thanks," Emma told her, still laughing as she pictured Billy trying to out eat his big brother Bobby.

It was exactly what Emma needed to get her mind off the fact that her dad was not coming tonight. Walking away quickly, Emma made her way to the gym. Finding a chair, Emma took her heels off and put on her tennis shoes. With her feet feeling better, Emma began getting everything ready for the pageant.

"What can we do to help?"

From up on a ladder, Emma turned around slowly to see who was talking to her. She spotted Jennifer and Sam.

"We're here to help," Jennifer announced.

"Thanks," Emma said, mentally listing what still needed to be done. "Jennifer, can you start by making sure we have all of the props in their proper place on the stage?"

"How do I know where they go?" Jennifer asked, heading for the back of the stage.

"There's a sign on each side of the stage saying which props are on which side," Emma explained.

"Great, I'm on it," Jennifer said, as she looked for the prop map.

"Sam, I need your help here," Emma said as she came down the ladder. "You're taller so could can you please change this light bulb? I think there are a couple more around the room that are out. Maintenance was going to do it, but I guess they forgot."

"I'll take care of it," Sam answered. "Are you okay? You seem on edge."

"Why would I be on edge," Emma snapped. "We're not ready and my dad is not coming."

"What do you mean your dad is not coming?" Sam asked looking at Emma in shock.

"Just what I said," Emma answered, her frustration reaching explosion levels. "I am trying to give him support, but tonight I could really use his and he won't be here!"

Turning around to keep herself from crying, Emma declared, "I can't talk about this anymore. I have to focus on what needs to be done here. Thanks for helping, Sam."

Emma quickly made her way back stage to find Jennifer laying out the props.

"Jenn, I need to talk to you," Emma said, knowing she had to vent these feelings or she was going to explode.

"Okay, but you'll have to do it while helping me move these chairs out of the way," Jennifer said without looking up from what she was doing. "I don't know what these chairs are doing back here anyway. I don't want any kid tripping over them."

Picking up a chair, Emma said sadly, "Dad's not coming tonight."

Stopping what she was doing, Jennifer turned to look at Emma and asked, "What do you mean Frank is not coming?"

As tears fell down her cheeks, Emma stomped her foot and said, "I am so angry! He never misses my pageants. He knows how important this pageant is to me, but he has to write one of his stupid Christmas Letters instead of coming."

Before she could say anymore, Jennifer stepped in, "Emma, stop!"

Surprised by her friend's response, Emma asked, "Are you going to stand here and take his side?"

"I am not on anyone's side, but if I have to pick, then yes, I am on your Dad's."

"Some friend you are," Emma said, her anger spewing over on Jennifer.

"That's right, I am," Jennifer told her, realizing exactly what Emma needed right now. "Since I am a good friend, I will be straight with you. First, you need to calm down and lower your voice. Everyone probably heard you say 'stupid Christmas Letters.' Second, this pageant is not about you. It's about your kids. So, stop your crying and start acting like the teacher your students love and put them first."

Emma was stunned, no one would ever speak to her that way except for Jennifer.

"Look, Emma," Jennifer said pulling her farther back behind the stage where no one could hear them. "I understand you wanting your dad here, but from what your mom has told me, you recently gave your dad your support and that made all the difference in the world. Now here you are, yelling and crying like a child because you did not get your way."

Calming down, Emma knew her friend was right. She felt ashamed at her angry outburst.

"And another thing," Jennifer said, looking her friend right in the eye. "If your dad says a letter has to go out first thing tomorrow, you have to know that this letter is extremely important. If it wasn't, he would be here now helping and cheering on your kids."

Emma nodded her head, hugged her friend, and whispered, "Thank you!"

Emma straightened her back determinedly and got busy with her duties as director. She said nothing else about her dad that evening. Jennifer was right, he would be here if he could and she owed her students her best because she knew that they would give their best tonight. Thinking about how hard her class had worked on this made Emma smile.

The pageant lasted about a half hour and was a huge success. Emma was so proud of her class. However, since her dad wasn't in the audience, she thanked Jennifer and Sam for their hard work with the pageant. Then she dedicated the pageant to her mom and thanked her for her support. The audience gave her mom a standing ovation and while her dad missed out, Emma knew it was one of the best pageants she's ever directed.

"Emma, it was amazing," Ruth said giving Emma big hug. "Great job!"

"Thanks, Mom," Emma smiled back.

Pulling her daughter aside, Ruth said, "I know you are disappointed that Dad missed the pageant, but you should be very proud of yourself."

"I am proud of my students!" Emma said with a broad smile.

"You had quite a cast this year," Ruth said.

"Well, with more kids, I had to be creative to find a place for all of them," Emma told her mom.

"Well, you did a great job at that," Ruth said sincerely. "The parents were thrilled with their performance. Now you can relax. How about some Christmas shopping tomorrow?"

"That would be great, but not too early," Emma said yawning. "This girl wants to sleep in."

"Why don't you come over around eleven and we'll get lunch and then hit the stores?" Ruth suggested.

"I'll be there," Emma smiled. "Thanks, Mom, for everything, are you ready to go?"

"Your Dad is picking me up," Ruth told her.

"I could have taken you home," Emma said.

"I know, but it's late and you and I have both had a very long day," Ruth said. "I want you to go straight home and get some sleep."

Hugging her mom, always made Emma feel better, "Thanks again, Mom. You are the best."

Emma took a deep breath and looked around the room to find only a few kids and parents left. They were speaking to Sam.

"You and the children did great," Jennifer said coming up behind her.

"Thanks, and thank you for all of your help and for straightening me out earlier," Emma said hugging her. "You truly are a great friend."

"You are welcome, any time," Jennifer said with a smile. "Now, I'm going to go home, kiss my husband and kids, and go to bed."

"You're not staying to close up?" Emma asked her.

"Nope, Sam has this and besides, this is one of the perks of being principal. Night," Jennifer smiled, waved, and walked off.

Emma started loading her car and by the third trip, she noticed that all the kids and parents were gone. *Finally, now I can go home,* she thought. Not seeing Sam, she reminded the maintenance people about turning off all of the lights when they closed up.

With her bag and one last box in her hands, she made her way to her car.

Sam saw her coming and reached for the box, "Can I help you with that?"

"Oh, I thought you already went home," Emma said with a smile.

"No, some of our parents like to talk," Sam said, wearily.

"Yes, they do," Emma agreed as she handed him the box. "You can just put the box back in the trunk with the rest of the boxes."

"So, why are you hanging around, aren't you tired?" Emma asked him.

"I'm exhausted, but I wanted to ask if you had plans tomorrow?" Sam asked her.

"I'm having lunch with my mom and then we are going Christmas shopping, why?" Emma asked.

"I was hoping you could help me finish decorating my house, but I can handle it," Sam explained. "You go have lunch and shop with your mom."

"I could ask her if we could shop then lunch and then I can come over in the afternoon," Emma offered.

"I don't want you to change your plans. I can handle this," Sam said.

"Are you sure?" Emma asked.

"Yes, go have fun with your mom," Sam answered.

"Okay, then good night Sam, thanks for your help tonight," Emma said as she got in her car. "See you Monday?"

"Monday or sooner," he said getting into his car.

I wonder what he meant by that? she asked herself as she turned up the music and sang all the way home to keep herself awake. Once she got home, she unloaded her car, made some hot chocolate, and sat in her window seat to wind down after her hectic, but successful evening.

The next morning, Emma rose earlier than she really wanted to, but she felt refreshed. She had a good night's sleep and was ready to tackle the day. She made herself a cup of coffee, sat into her window seat and thought about last night, how her dad had missed the show, and how she acted in front of Jennifer.

Shaking her head sadly, she thought, *I hope no one saw me having a temper tantrum last night.*

After breakfast, Emma really didn't know what to do with herself since she was not due at her parents' house until eleven o'clock. *I wonder if Sam would like help now*, she thought. *It's early, though, and he might still be sleeping.* Pacing her living room, Emma thought about texting him, but she didn't want to wake him.

"Are you up?" she texted.

He did not text right back. *I guess he is still sleeping, which is a good thing. I wish I was!*

Her phone went off, "Yes, I'm up, what's wrong?"

She texted back, "Nothing, I was just wondering if you would like to meet for breakfast?"

Emma waited and waited wondering what was taking him so long to answer a simple question.

"Yes, what time?" he texted.

"In an hour at the diner?" she responded.

"OK," he wrote back and that was that.

Emma dressed and made it to the diner before Sam. Sitting at the counter, she ordered hot chocolate with marshmallows. *I wonder what is taking him so long,* she thought, but just when she was about to text him, he walked in. He looked tired and she realized he must have been asleep and she woke him.

"Hi, sorry I'm late," Sam smiled.

"Did I wake you? Don't lie to me," Emma asked.

Smiling, Sam gave a little nod.

"I am so sorry," Emma apologized. "Why didn't you tell me? We did not have to meet?"

"I had the same idea, I was just going to do it a little later when it was actually daybreak," he said and they both laughed.

"I must have slept so well that once I woke up, I couldn't go back to sleep," Emma explained. "Since I dragged you out of bed, I'm buying."

"Emma, you don't have to," Sam smiled at her.

"I know, but I want to, so what will you have?" she said firmly, smiling.

During breakfast, Sam and Emma reminisced about how wonderful the pageant was and for some reason Emma even told him about her blow up in front of Jennifer.

"That must have been some scene," Sam said to her.

"It was! Jennifer really let me have it, for which I am very grateful," Emma told him. "She has no problem putting me in my place when needed."

"Only a good friend would do that," Sam said trying to cover his yawn.

As Sam and Emma ate, their talk turned to Thanksgiving and the holidays.

"When are your parents coming into town?" Emma asked him.

"Tomorrow, that's why I have to finish up my decorating," Sam explained.

"I thought we already did that," Emma said wondering what more needed to be done.

"We did, but I am putting a couple of final touches in their bedroom and bathroom," Sam answered.

"I'm sure you will do great," encouraged Emma.

"Thanks, so where are you having lunch with your mom?" Sam asked.

"I don't know, maybe here," she said and they both laughed.

"Are you sure you are going to be hungry after that big breakfast?" Sam asked.

"I'll probably just get a salad," Emma responded. "I better be going, though."

"Thanks for breakfast and enjoy your day with your mom," Sam said.

When Emma got to her Mom's, her Dad was at his desk as usual.

Knocking on his door, she walked in and said, "Hi, Dad!"

"Emma," he said getting up from behind his desk. "I'm sorry I missed the pageant last night."

"It's okay, but please don't make a habit of missing them," she told him.

"I won't, I promise," he said giving her a hug. "You and your mom are off shopping today, right?"

"Yes, lunch then shopping or shopping then dinner," Emma told him. "I don't know which."

Turning to leave then stopping at the door she asked, "How's the new pen?"

"It's great, and it doesn't seem to take a lot of ink which is good," he said with a smile.

"Emma, there you are," her mom appeared at the door. "You ready to go?"

"I am," Emma said then asked, "How hungry are you?"

"Why?" Ruth asked smiling.

"Well, I had breakfast with Sam so I'm really not hungry yet, but if you are we'll go eat."

"I'm fine," Ruth said smiling. "Your dad and I slept in and we just finished breakfast a little while ago. Let's shop and then you can come back here for dinner."

"Sounds good," Emma agreed.

They shopped for nearly four hours and that was all Emma could handle, "Mom, I'm done. I think we have bought out the entire store."

She put the last bag into her trunk and said, "I am glad I took out the boxes from the pageant last night or we wouldn't have any room for all of that you bought."

"I think I have made a good dent into my Christmas shopping this year and you didn't do so bad yourself," Ruth said.

"No, I got what I needed," Emma agreed.

As the women hopped into Emma's car, they turned on their seat heaters. It had turned very cold.

"They are predicting snow showers for Thanksgiving," Ruth said.

"I hope they are right," Emma smiled. "I have been praying for snow this year and we might actually get it."

When they reached Ruth's house, Emma helped carry in her mom's bags and went in to check on her Dad. She was about to knock, but she could see that he was sound asleep sitting in his chair.

Going back into the kitchen, her Mom asked her, "Did you tell your dad we were here?"

"I was going to, but he's asleep," Emma answered.

"He's been doing that a lot lately," Ruth told Emma.

"Sleeping?" Emma asked.

"Taking naps during the day," Ruth said.

"What's up with that? Dad has never taken naps," Emma stated.

"Well, he's got a lot on his mind and his letters are taking a toll this year," Ruth said, sounding a bit concerned.

"What do you mean a 'taking a toll'?" Emma asked, looking at her Mom.

"He's fine. It's just he's a little more stressed than usual," Ruth said trying to sound more nonchalant. "He told me not to worry and that he's fine, so I dropped it."

"Mom, maybe Dad needs to take it easy and not write so many," Emma suggested.

"Don't let him hear you say that," her mom cautioned her.

"I mean it," Emma said firmly. "Dad needs to take care of himself."

"He is," Ruth told her.

"Really, Mom?" she questioned.

"Yes, Emma, I know how to take care of your dad," Ruth said sternly. "I have been doing this for over forty years now. Please set the table and help me get the food ready."

Emma smiled knowing her mom was done discussing this. She said nothing more and when dinner was ready Emma walked into her Dad's office.

It looked like he had just awakened, "Hey, when did you all get back?"

"A while ago, but you were sleeping so we didn't want to wake you," Emma answered. "Dad, are you sure you're alright? You never take naps."

"This time of year, I do," he laughed and then asked, "Is dinner ready?"

"Yes," Emma told him, so they headed for the kitchen.

During dinner, Emma could not bring herself to speak about the pageant for she still had Jennifer's words engraved in her head.

"If you ladies will excuse me, I'm going back to work," her dad said.

"You haven't had dessert yet," Ruth said.

"I'll have it later," he said as he got up, kissed Ruth, and went into his office.

"I'll bring you a piece of pie later," she yelled after him.

As Emma and her mom cleared the dishes, "You seem quiet, Emma, are you alright?"

"I'm fine, Mom," Emma said.

"No, you're up to something," her mom said.

Putting down the kitchen towel and kissing her mom on the cheek, Emma made her way down to her dad's office.

When she knocked, her dad invited her to come in, "Are you and your mom done with the dishes?"

"Yes, Dad, so can I talk to you a minute?" Emma asked.

"Sure," he responded putting down the antique pen. "Emma, I have to say, I am so thankful to Sam for giving me this beautiful pen."

"I'm so glad you like your pen," Emma said softly as she sat down and leaned forward, putting her elbows on her knees. "So, who's letter did you have to write last night?"

"I was wondering when we were going to talk about this. I have to admit I am surprised we didn't discuss this at dinner," her dad said looking her in the eyes.

"I didn't want to upset Mom," Emma said. "So, who's letter was so important that you had to get it out today?"

"You know I can't tell you that," he said holding his hand up to stop Emma from speaking, "but I can tell you it went to a couple who goes to our church."

"Now, how about dessert?" her Dad said as he started to get up.

"Couldn't you have written this letter this morning?" Emma asked, tears starting to fill Emma's eyes and shaking her head. "You still don't know do you?"

"Know what?" he asked.

"Since I decided to give my support to your Christmas Letters this year, I was dedicating this year's pageant to you, Dad. You should have been there," Emma sobbed. "It makes me wonder how many other pageants are you going to miss?"

"Emma, I already said I was sorry, what more do you want me to say?" her dad asked.

"You know how important these pageants are to me," she pouted.

"I do," her Dad said sternly, "but sometimes you have to put others before yourself, Emma."

"I'm not heartless, but you can see why I have a problem with this, right?" Emma asked, raising her voice. "You always put these letters before me and mom!"

Storming out and grabbing her coat, she called out, "Mom, I'm sorry but I just can't stay."

"Emma, it's not all about you," her Dad yelled from the doorway of his office.

This was the third time she had heard those exact same words in less than twenty-four hours.

"Your mother understands, why can't you?" her Dad yelled after her.

That had done it! She was angry and hurt. It took everything out of her to keep her mouth shut so she wouldn't say something she would surely regret. Saying nothing, she reached for the front door and walked out, got into her car, and drove home with no radio and no music—just agonizing silence.

Once she reached her condo, Emma ran up the stairs, opened the door, walked into her bedroom, and collapsed on her bed crying.

Chapter 6

The next morning, Emma noticed that she had fallen asleep with her clothes on and tears began to fall. Emma could still hear her Dad's words echoing over and over again in her head.

She made her way over to her window seat after she made herself a cup of coffee and looked up.

"I'm sorry. I don't know what to do," she whispered with tears in her eyes.

Emma sat for quite a while until she was ready to face Dad once more.

Feeling guilty, Emma made her way to her parents' home. Instead of turning up the Christmas music, Emma turned off the radio. No music could ease the pain she was feeling. When she arrived at her parents' home, Emma didn't even glance over at Sam's house. He was the farthest thing from her mind. In fact, she wondered what she was going to walk into once she entered her parents' home.

Knocking softly, Emma entered and called out softly, "Hello?"

"We're in here," her mom roared.

Emma knew she was in trouble, not only for yelling at her Dad, but disrespecting both of her parents. With her stomach in a knot, Emma made her way into the kitchen.

Ruth was standing at the counter and her Dad was sitting at the kitchen table reading the morning paper.

Her Dad glanced over at his daughter and a slight smile came to his face he said, "Hi, Emma."

"I am so sorry for the way I acted last night. I had no right," Emma began.

"No, you didn't," her mom scolded. "Sit down, Emma."

Ruth pointed and Emma sat down next to her Dad.

"I am so tired of the both of you," Ruth yelled. "Frank, you could have written that letter this morning, but you chose not to causing you to miss the pageant; the one event Emma asks you to attend every year."

Emma could not believe what she was hearing. Her Mom was scolding her Dad instead of her! A little smile came to her face, but it soon faded as her mom turned to her.

"And Emma, you had no right to speak to us the way you did. Don't ever disrespect us ever again," her mother said firmly.

Emma nodded her head for she could not bear to look at her Mom. She had hurt both of them terribly.

"I am sick of both of you acting like children," her mother said angrily. "Frank, it's time, you explain why you write the Christmas Letters, and Emma, you are going to listen. Then I don't want to hear another word about the Christmas Letters ever again!"

"Emma, these letters are important, and you will respect me and your Dad. Frank, family is more important than any letter.

Do you both understand me?" Ruth yelled. "Now get out of my sight, both of you!"

Emma had never seen her mom so angry.

Her Dad got up from the table, went over and hugged and kissed his wife, then said softly, "I'll explain."

Emma turned and she saw her Dad getting his coat.

"Emma, let's go," he said looking back at her.

"Where are we going?" Emma asked as she made her way down to the front door.

Emma heard her Mom's voice call from the kitchen, "I love you both, but sometimes you make it difficult."

Frank and Emma smiled as they walked to Emma's car.

As Emma turned on her Christmas music, her dad said softly, "Not too loud, please."

As they listened to the music, neither one spoke. Emma wondered where they were going as she pulled out onto the street.

"Make a left at the next light," her dad instructed.

When Emma turned the corner, she saw their church down the street and asked, "Are we going to the church?"

Her Dad did not answer, but motioned for her to pull into the church parking lot.

Emma asked, "Dad, why are we at church?"

"Let's go inside," Frank said as he got out of her car and walked toward the front door.

Emma quietly followed her Dad as they swiftly walked into their church. "I don't think I have ever been in here when it was so quiet," she said.

"I know what you mean," her Dad said with a smile. "Emma, come up to the front with me."

When they reached the front, Frank asked her, "What do you see?"

Emma looked around and answered, "I see the altar and the cross."

"And what does that cross mean to you?" Frank asked as he sat in the second row on the end facing the altar.

Emma looking up at the cross turned around and faced her Dad saying, "That Jesus died on the cross for my sins."

Sitting down in front of her dad, she turned around to face him and asked, "Where are you going with this, Dad?"

Leaning back in his chair, he asked yet another question, "When you see Jesus up on that cross, what does that mean to you?"

"That He died for us," Emma answered.

"Jesus dying on that cross was a gift to us, right?" Frank continued.

Emma nodded her head, but as she started to ask what Jesus dying on the cross had to do with his Christmas Letters, Frank raised up his right hand and asked, "Emma, why do we celebrate Christmas?"

Getting frustrated, Emma answered, "We are celebrating the birth of Jesus, of course."

"That's right," her dad said patiently. "So, if God has given us the gift of His Only Son, knowing that someday He would have to be put to death for our sins, don't you think we should give a gift back to Him?"

Emma felt her stomach drop and for a moment, she did not know what to say. She tried to talk, but no words came to mind.

Her dad continued, "Christmas is about giving not receiving and that is what I am doing with the Christmas Letters I write. I am giving back something to God because of what He gave to me."

"Dad," Emma said, clearing her throat, "How do you know who should receive a letter?"

"That is a conversation for another time, but know this, not everyone has a family like ours where there is love, peace, and understanding," he said with a smile. "What we have is a blessing and it's our responsibility to help those in need."

"I understand about helping others and you're right, we should help those in need and not just at Christmas," Emma agreed. "So, why do you only write at Christmas?"

Leaning toward his daughter, he spoke quietly saying, "Because at Christmas, I am reminded of the huge sacrifice Christ made for me. I choose to celebrate His birth by helping others. I need to give back because of what Jesus did for me and for our family."

Turning to look directly into her eyes, he asked, "Emma, do you understand?"

"I think so," Emma nodded. "That is why I became a teacher. I like to help others, too, but Dad, you could write your letters at a different time, like in the Spring around Easter when we celebrate Jesus' resurrection."

Frank sat back thinking his daughter had a point, "I could and I do write throughout the year, but at Christmas it seems more people need something extra."

Thinking back to why he and Ruth started writing the Christmas Letters was not something he wanted to get into with Emma today, he asked, "Am I making any sense?"

Tears began to fall down Emma's cheeks. As she wiped her eyes, she moved to the next row and sat down next to her dad.

Grabbing his left hand, she said softly, "I'm sorry, Dad, I still don't quite understand. Something tells me there is more to this, but I won't push. You're right our family is blessed and at Christmas we should give back more. I wish I could give back more."

"Emma, you do in your own way, but if you really believe that that you need to talk to Him, pointing to the cross" he smiled and stood up.

Emma did not know what to say, but she knew her Dad's words would stay with her.

"Can we go home now?" he asked with a smile.

"Not just yet, Dad, I need you to hear me," Emma said, carefully choosing her next words.

As Frank sat back down and turned toward his daughter, Emma began, "I'm sorry I haven't respected your writings. I now understand why you write them, but it's just that I miss you and I wish we spent more time together during the holidays."

Emma's voice cracked and tears began to fall again.

Trying to compose herself, she attempted to continue, "Do you remember when all of us would sit in your living room and Ben would start a fire as Mom and I would make hot chocolate? Then we would watch White Christmas together. How long has it been since we've done that?"

Frank shook his head and said nothing for he could not remember.

"We rarely see you. Year after year, it is the same thing. Mom and I watch our favorite Christmas movie and you stay in your office," Emma said shaking her head sadly. "Dad, nobody is guaranteed tomorrow and I would hate to see you look back and say. 'I wish I would have spent more time with my family during Christmas.' We all miss you including Ben and Cathy and the boys. Can you tell me that you don't miss us at Christmas?"

Frank could not speak as he wondered how long it had been since he watched White Christmas with his family. *I think Nathan was just born*, he thought to himself. He always thought that he was doing what God called him to do, but Emma just reminded him that he needed to pray about his calling. He, too, was starting to wonder if he is supposed to carry on with the Christmas Letters.

"I do miss you, but I don't know of any other way to write them," Frank admitted softly. "It takes a lot of time and I have to do what I am called to do."

"Yes you do," Emma agreed. "So, let me ask you this, do you think God would want you to neglect your family even when He has called you to do something for Him?"

"Do you really feel neglected?" Frank asked, surprised that was how she was feeling.

"I do in a way," Emma said, gently putting her hand on her Dad's back. "Dad, I love you and I miss you during the holidays."

Emma stood, but sat back down seeing her Dad was deep in thought, "Do you remember when I was in Florida and the only way I saw you and Mom was when you came to see me? Well, you gave me some great advice then that I have never forgotten. Do you remember what you told me?"

"No, I can't say that I do," Frank admitted, staring at the altar.

"You told me that life is precious and that each day is a gift because no one is guaranteed tomorrow," Emma told him, clearly remembering the day he said those words to her. "Dad, look at me, do what you are called to do but don't ever forget your family. Remember, each day is a gift."

Frank wiped the tears from his eyes, "Emma, I know but I have to write my Christmas Letters and I don't know of any other way to write them."

"Let Mom and me help you," Emma said, surprising herself by what she was saying.

At this point, she was willing to do anything to have her Dad back.

However, her dad shook his head and said, "No, this is my project and you and your Mom do not have the time to help."

Emma could not believe how her Dad's perspective had changed so quickly.

"Emma, think about it, do you have time with your schedule? I know your Mom doesn't. Christmas is a very busy time for all of us," he said.

"Yes, but Mom and I would make time for you because we are family," Emma said sincerely.

"I appreciate it, I really do," Frank said firmly. "But this is something I have to do."

Emma knew there was no use talking to him about this anymore. His mind was made up.

"Let's go home," he said as he stood and starting walking toward the door. Emma knew their conversation was over.

As they walked out of the church, a chill came over them. They walked silently down the steps of their church and made their way out toward the church parking lot.

"Let's race," her Dad said mischievously and they both started running.

Frank didn't see the patch of ice that had formed at the rear of Emma's car and before she could reach out and grab a hold of her dad, he was down on the pavement clutching his right arm.

Chapter 7

"Dad, are you okay?" Emma asked worriedly.

"I'll be alright, but you need to get me to the hospital. I think I broke my arm," he said clutching his arm.

"Did you hit your head?" Emma asked, sounding just like her mom.

"No!" Frank said as he tried to stand without using his arm.

"Don't move. I'm calling an ambulance," Emma said, quickly reaching for her phone.

"No need, just get me up and help me into your car," he told her.

"I'm not moving you," Emma said, dialing 911.

"Hi, my name is Elizabeth Trask. My Dad and I are in the parking lot of First Baptist Church, and we need an ambulance. My dad just fell on the ice and broke his arm."

Responding to the dispatcher, Emma answered, "No, he did not hit his head. Thank you."

Kneeling down beside her dad, she said, "They'll be here soon."

"You better call your Mom," he told her.

"I will as soon as the paramedics get here," Emma said as the tears started to form in her eyes. "Dad, this is my fault. I didn't even see the ice, I'm sorry."

"Not your fault," Frank said shaking his head. "I'm the one who wanted to run. I should have known there would be ice from last night."

"Where are they?" Emma said impatiently as she stood up looking around.

"Emma, I'm going to be fine," he said, but Emma could tell her Dad was trying to put on a brave face for she knew his arm was hurting.

Emma knelt down again beside him, "Dad, does anything else hurt?"

Trying to smile, he said ruefully, "Just my pride."

"Where are they?" Emma said again, wanting to get her dad up off the cold ground.

"They will be here soon," Frank said. "You need to stay calm so you can call your mother."

"I am calm," she said. "I just want to get you out of the cold and into the ambulance."

"Wait, I think I hear them," Frank said, obviously relieved.

Standing up, Emma said, "Yes, I can see them. I am going to go over by the entrance and flag them down."

Emma walked quickly toward the entrance of the church, watching where she was going just in case there was another patch of ice.

"Over here!" she yelled, waving wildly.

Seeing they were heading toward her, Emma walked back over to where her Dad was leaning back against her car. *There is no way he will be able to write those letters now*, she thought. *That is going to crush Dad, but I can't think about that now. I need to get him to the hospital.* Her Dad did not look well at all.

While the paramedics were getting out their equipment and a gurney, Emma bent down and kissed her Dad on top of his head and said, "I love you, Dad!"

"I love you, too," he said trying to smile. "It's going to be alright."

"I will call Mom once they tell me how you are doing and where they are taking you," she said trying to hold back her tears.

Backing out of the way so the paramedics could check out her Dad, tears started to well up in Emma's eyes. Quickly pushing them away, *keep it together Emma*, she said to herself.

It seemed to take the paramedics a long time to check her dad out and just when Emma was about to say something, they said, "We're ready to take him to the hospital."

"Is he alright?" Emma asked, concerned they had found something more than a broken arm.

"His vitals are good, though his blood pressure is elevated, and he definitely has a broken arm," one of them answered her.

"I told her that she could take me," her dad told them.

"No, Mr. Trask, your daughter did the right thing, by calling for us," the paramedic said.

"Dad, I'm going to go get Mom and we will meet you at the hospital, okay?" Emma asked him.

"Thanks, Emma," Frank said. "Tell her not to worry."

The two paramedics lifted Frank onto the gurney and then put him into the ambulance while Emma stood and answered questions and signed paperwork.

"Your Dad is going to be fine, but he does need x-rays and a cast on that arm," they assured her. "Are you alright to drive? Do you need to call someone to come and get you?"

"I'm fine. I'm going to go pick up my Mom and then we will come to the hospital," Emma assured them.

"Drive careful and when you get to the hospital, just follow the signs to the emergency entrance," they told her.

"Thank you," Emma said then watched the ambulance drive away.

For a moment, Emma seemed paralyzed and could not move. When she could no longer see it, she looked at the frozen puddle where her Dad had fallen and the tears fell down her face.

This is all my fault! she said to herself.

As she got behind the wheel of her car, tears again began to fill her eyes. Determinedly wiping them away, she willed herself to calm down, so she could call her Mom.

Still shaking, she said, "Mom, there has been an accident. Dad fell on some ice at church and broke his right arm. I called an ambulance and he is on his way to the emergency room. I am on my way to get you. I'll be there soon and will explain everything."

As Emma drove to her Mom's house, she turned down the music and tried to pray, but the image of what just happened kept playing over and over in her head. She also knew her Mom would want to know every detail of what happened. When she pulled in her parent's driveway, Ruth was standing outside waiting for her.

As soon as she got in, she said, "Emma, what happened and don't leave anything out."

Backing out of the driveway, Emma started to tell her Mom about their visit to the church and that they had a good conversation. Then she told her Mom that when they were leaving her dad wanted to race to the car and didn't see the patch of ice.

"He tried to slow himself down, but it happened so fast that he went down. I couldn't reach him in time to break his fall, Mom," she said sadly, tears threatening to start again.

"Emma, it's not your fault," Ruth told her.

"Yes, it is," Emma said. "If I would not have acted the way I did and just supported him like I said I would, none of this would have happened."

Feeling the tears well up again, Emma quickly wiped her hand over her cheek and drove to the hospital.

Her Mom sat quietly beside her. Emma hated it when her Mom was silent. It just wasn't in her nature. Glancing at her Mom, there was no smile just silence which made her wonder what her Mom was thinking.

Ruth actually agreed with Emma that if she would have supported her Dad like she said she would none of this would have happened. However, Ruth loved her daughter and knew that everything happens for a reason. Knowing how bad her daughter felt, Ruth reached out her hand and tapped Emma's leg.

"Emma, this was an accident," Ruth said gently. "You are not to blame. Your Dad should know that running at his age is never a good idea even under the best of conditions."

As Emma pulled up to the emergency entrance, Ruth immediately jumped out of the car and went quickly inside.

"I'll meet you inside," Emma said, but her Mom was already in the doors.

As Emma watched the emergency doors closing behind her Mom, tears fell down her face. After she parked her car, she looked in the rearview mirror and said a little prayer.

Taking a deep breath, Emma got out of the car just as her phone rang, "Hello, Sam! Sorry, I can't talk now. I will call you later."

Emma quickly hung up and made her way to the emergency entrance. Walking into the hospital and up to the information desk, Emma impatiently stood in line to talk to the nurse who was on the phone.

"Excuse me, can you tell me where Frank Trask is?" Emma asked another nurse passing by.

"I don't know, mam, you will have to wait until she gets off the phone and she will help you."

Emma stood in line for what seemed like forever. Unable to wait any longer, she jumped out of line and started walking down the hall, peeking behind curtains in search of her parents.

"Emma?" she heard a voice behind her.

"Are you Emma Trask?" a nurse asked her.

"Yes," Emma answered, concerned they were looking for her.

"Follow me," the nurse said.

Emma walked behind the nurse to the end of the hall, where she was relieved to see her Dad sitting up in the hospital bed.

"Dad, where's Mom?" she asked him.

"She's supposed to be filling out paperwork," Frank answered.

"I didn't see her," Emma told him.

"Emma, please go look for her," Frank asked.

Leaving her purse, Emma started down the hall and found her Mom, sitting in what looked like a very uncomfortable chair, filling out paperwork,

"Mom, I found Dad," Emma told her.

"Good! I haven't seen him yet," Ruth said disgustedly. "Why do they have you fill out so many papers when you come in?"

"Can't I do it for you?" Emma asked.

"No, but will you please go check on your Dad?" Ruth said.

"I was just there and he sent me to find you," Emma smiled.

"I'm almost done, so will you please just go sit with him until I get there?" her Mom asked impatiently.

"Sure, Mom, Dad's room is all the way down the hall, last door on the left," Emma told her Mom, giving her a hug. "He's going to be fine."

"I'm sorry, Emma," her Mom apologized. "I just need a doctor to tell me he's alright."

As Emma made her way down to her Dad's room, she spotted him on a gurney being pushed down the hallway.

Running up to him, she asked, "What's wrong?"

"Nothing, they are going to take me down for an x-ray of my arm," Frank told her. "I will be back in a few minutes.

"Then I want to go home," he said turning around looking at the nurse pushing him.

"I know you want to go home, Mr. Trask," she smiled patiently. "But we need to know how much damage you have done to that arm."

"Well then, let's get a move on," Frank demanded.

Emma looked at the nurse and mouthed, "Sorry!"

The nurse smiled back.

"Okay," tapping her Dad's shoulder. "I'll let Mom know what's going on."

With her Dad gone, Emma turned around, walked into the empty room, sat in the chair, and started to cry.

"What's wrong?" a sharp anxious voice startled Emma.

"Oh, Mom, nothing is wrong," Emma said wiping the tears from her eyes.

"Where's Dad?"

"He went to go get an x-ray of his arm," Emma explained. "Mom, are you alright?"

"No, you scared me," Ruth said, taking a deep shaky breath and sitting down in the chair Emma had been sitting in. "I came in, your Dad was missing, and you were crying. I was afraid something had happened!"

Giving her Mom a hug, Emma said, "I'm sorry, Mom. Dad's fine, he's insisting he's fine and he keeps telling the nurses that he wants to go home."

"Your Dad is not a very good patient," Ruth smiled knowingly. "The way he is acting, I am sure they will want to get rid of him."

Emma knew her Mom was not going to relax until she saw her husband and knew he was going to be alright.

Emma jumped when her phone went off in her pocket, "Hello? Oh, hi Sam."

She walked out into the hall, "Sorry I haven't called you back. Dad fell on some ice when he and I were at church earlier. We're at the hospital now. I have to go now, but I'll call you later when I have more details."

Emma could see her Dad on a stretcher coming down the hall and he was not smiling.

"How are you Frank?" her Mom asked anxiously.

"I'm fine, Ruth. It's just a broken arm," he told her. "I know what you are thinking and you're right, I should not have been running."

Bending over and kissing her husband, she said, "Actually I was thinking that I am so grateful that you are okay. What did the doctor say?"

"Not much," Frank said disgustedly. "He said he would come back when he had all of the test and x-ray results. Hopefully, he'll be here soon. I want to go home."

"Frank, I know. Now try to relax," Ruth told him.

"Ruth...."

"I know, Frank, but maybe it isn't as bad as you think," Ruth said.

Emma could not follow what her parents were saying. They seem to have a code between them that she could not figure out.

Within fifteen minutes, the doctor walked in and introduced himself, "Hi, I'm doctor Ezekiel, but you can call me Dr. Zeke. Frank, how are you doing?"

"My arm hurts and I want to go home," Frank said firmly.

"I'm sure it does and I am sure you do. In fact, I hear you have been a little grumpy with my nurses," the doctor said trying to maintain a firm look on his face.

"Frank, really!" Ruth scolded.

"I'm sorry, but I'm feeling very foolish," Frank said sheepishly. "Of all the stupid things to do, I tried to race my daughter to the car knowing we had freezing temperatures last night."

"Frank, take it easy," Dr. Zeke said. "I will give you something for the pain and if you are up to it, you can go home or would you rather spend the night?"

The look on Frank's face made everybody in the room laugh.

"Very funny, Doc!" Frank said.

"I'm sorry, Frank, but you have to admit it was funny," Dr. Zeke said smiling. "It made your wife and your daughter smile."

Trying to shake the doctor's hand, Frank looked right at him and said, "Thank you, Dr. Ezekiel."

"You are welcome," the doctor replied. "I will see you in a couple of days."

"Why a couple of days?" Emma asked.

The doctor turned and looked at Emma, "This is a temporary cast. In a couple of days, you will need to be fitted with a cast. Cheer up, though, Frank, you can still eat Thanksgiving dinner with your left hand."

"How long will he be in the cast?" Emma asked.

"Six to eight weeks," Dr. Zeke told them. "In six weeks, we'll take an x-ray and if it's all healed we'll take it off then, and if it still needs more time to heal, we'll wait until eight weeks."

The doctor could tell this was not good news for the Trask family.

"Listen, it is just a fracture. Frank, you will heal and I'm sure your wife will take care of you," the doctor said encouragingly.

"Oh, I intend to. Thank you, Dr. Ezekiel," Ruth said.

"Not a problem, Happy Thanksgiving," the doctor smiled and left.

"Emma, you might as well go home, the discharge could take a while," Ruth told her.

"I'm staying, but I am going to call Jennifer and Sam and let them know what happened," Emma said.

"Good idea," Ruth agreed. "Please call Jennifer first and let her know I will not be in on Monday."

"Ruth, you can go to work, I'll be fine," Frank told her.

"I'm staying home and I don't want to hear any more about it," Ruth told him in her no-nonsense voice.

Emma went out into the hall and called Jennifer and told her about their visit to the church, their race, and the fall.

"I am so sorry Emma!" Jennifer said sincerely. "Do you want to take the day off, too? I can get a temp for your class?"

"I want to, but Mom already is, so I'm going to come to work," Emma told Jennifer.

"I love your Dad, but what was he thinking wanting to race?" Jennifer asked.

"Jenn, it happened so fast, I couldn't catch him," tears fell down Emma's face again.

"Emma, it's not your fault. Now, you stop it," Jenn said firmly. "Your parents need you to be strong."

"You're right as usual," Emma told her friend. "I'll see you tomorrow. I'll stop by your office first thing in the morning and let you know how things are going."

Emma hung up the phone with Jennifer and then she called Sam.

"Hi Sam, it's me. Dad broke his arm while we were in the church parking lot earlier," Emma explained. "Mom and I are at the hospital. I just wanted you to know."

"I'll be right there, Emma," Sam said compassionately.

"No, really you don't have to," Emma said.

"I'm coming," Sam said firmly.

"Fine, I'll see you soon then, thanks," Emma said, secretly glad he was coming.

She hung up the phone and walked down to her Dad's room. Her Dad had tears in his eyes which was a first. She had never seen her Dad cry before.

"What's wrong?" Emma asked, wondering what could have happened the short time it took her to make those two phone calls.

When Ruth wiped the tears from her face as well, Emma asked again, "What's wrong? Dad answer me!"

"I can't write, Emma," her Dad said sadly.

"Dad, it's okay, Mom can write out the bills," Emma assured him.

"But I can't write my Christmas Letters," Frank said with tears in his eyes.

"I know and I'm sorry, but maybe it's for the best," Emma said.

Frank and Ruth said nothing.

"Emma, you need to go home. We'll talk tomorrow," Ruth told her.

"No, I want to stay. Dad, you are going to be alright, it's just a broken arm," Emma said. "I understand that you're upset about the letters, but there is always next year. I am sure God will understand. Maybe this is His way of telling you that you should retire."

Realizing what she had just said, Emma knew she should not have said it.

"Hi," a voice, came up behind Emma.

"Sam," Ruth said, "Good to see you."

"How did you get here that quickly?" asked Emma, grateful for the interruption.

"I was already here," Sam said. "When you called me, I was just pulling into the parking lot. So how are you, Frank?"

"He broke his arm and he is going to be in a permanent cast for at least six weeks maybe longer," Ruth answered.

"I'm sorry, Frank," Sam told him. "Ruth, is there anything I can do?"

"Yes, can you please take Emma home?" Ruth asked. "It's going to be a while before we can leave."

"Mom, I want to stay," Emma said. "Besides, my car is here."

"Emma, please, we just want to be alone," Ruth said.

"I'm sorry, but I don't understand why you both are mad at me," Emma said.

Frank raised his voice, "Sam, please get her out of here!"

Chapter 8

"Emma, let's go," Sam said as he gently pushed Emma out into the hallway.

"What's going on with them?" Sam asked when he was sure they couldn't hear him.

Emma, obviously annoyed, stood with her arms folded and answered, "My Dad took a bad fall and thankfully his only injury is a broken arm. You would think that they would be grateful. This fall could have been so much worse and all they can think about are those precious Christmas Letters."

"Sam, when Dad fell, it really scared me!" she said as the tears came.

This time, she couldn't hold them back any longer.

Sam took her in his arms, "Emma, what's important now is that I take you home."

Pulling herself back from him, "No, I have my car, I can drive myself."

"Doesn't your Mom need it to take your dad home?" Sam asked.

"She doesn't really like to drive it, so she'll call me or someone from the church to come and get them," Emma said. "Besides I need my car."

"I'll follow you," Sam said firmly.

"No need," Emma said as she turned and walked out to her car.

Getting into her car, Emma looked at herself in the rear-view mirror.

"Girl, you look awful!" she told her reflection.

She turned up her music and pulled out of the emergency entrance parking lot.

When they reached her condo, Emma got out and walked up to Sam who had pulled in right behind her.

"You don't listen!" she accused him. "I told you I can get home all by myself."

"Emma, you're upset," Sam said gently.

"You think!" she said sarcastically. "My Dad broke his right arm, his writing arm!"

"I know," Sam said. "Come on, let's go inside. You must be exhausted."

Emma nodded as she and Sam walked up to her condo. Once inside, Emma took off her coat and plopped down on her couch with her arms folded angrily across her body.

Looking up at Sam, she asked, "Why didn't you back me up at the hospital?"

"It's not my place," Sam said. "Besides, I didn't want to make your dad any more upset."

"It's only a broken arm, yet he and Mom are acting like this is the worst thing that could ever happen to Dad," Emma said shaking her head.

"Emma, it's his writing arm," Sam said quietly. "You know how important those Christmas Letters are to him."

"Yes, I do," Emma told him. "In fact, he and I had a conversation earlier at the church."

Emma stood up and started pacing as she thought about her conversation with her Dad.

"I even offered to help, but he didn't want my help," Emma told Sam. "I told him I was sorry for not supporting him and would from now on."

Calmer now, Emma continued, "Then he challenged me to a race in the parking lot, fell and broke his right arm, and now he can't write them. If he doesn't want Mom and my help, he won't be able to send them out this year."

"You could show your Dad some compassion," Sam suggested, regretting it the minute he said it.

Turning around angrily so she faced Sam, she said, "Compassion? I understand more than you know. His Christmas Letters are important and have meaning, but under the circumstances he should be more concerned about his health than writing those letters."

Tearing up again she said, "That fall could have been...,"

Stopping herself from putting into words what she had been thinking ever since her dad's fall, she said, "I'm tired of talking about this."

Emma made her way to her window seat and sat down wearily, "Sam, I need you to help me convince my Dad that he needs to give up writing these Christmas Letters."

"No, Emma," Sam said shaking his head. "I can't do that."

"Why not?" Emma asked, hurt by his response.

"Because it is not my place," Sam said. "I don't think he should give it up and neither should you."

"Okay, let me explain," Emma said. "This could be sign from God that He wants Dad to give up his writing. In fact, the more I think about it the more I'm convinced that this is a sign. Now he'll be able to spend more time with Mom, me, and the rest of the family."

"Do you hear yourself, Emma?" Sam asked. "Do you still want your Dad to stop doing what he loves and what he is called to do?"

"I am convinced more than ever that he should stop writing all together!" Emma said firmly.

"I have to go," Sam said as he quickly turned and walked out the door.

"Sam," Emma yelled after him.

"Goodbye, Emma, I can't listen to this anymore," Sam said walking quickly to his car. "Get some rest. You are obviously not thinking clearly."

Emma watched Sam drive away, then she shut the door and went to bed. After tossing and turning for over an hour, Emma got up, made herself a cup of hot chocolate, and curled up in her window seat.

"Dad does need to give this up," she said out loud. "Then he'll spend more time with us during the holidays."

However, as Emma stared out into the night, she thought, *who am I kidding? With his arm broken, Dad will be moping around and will make Mom and everyone else miserable.*

I did say I would help with the letters but Dad was right, though, Mom and I can't do it. She has enough on her plate, and I have the Christmas staff party to coordinate, Christmas shopping, decorating, and papers to grade. I do not have time to write letters to strangers that I do not even know. Dad will just have to wait until next year to write again, Emma continued, convincing herself until she felt she was right.

Emma went back to bed thinking she had it all settled in her mind, but she tossed all night. When she finally got up, her conscience had gotten the best of her.

Making her way over into her kitchen, she made herself a cup of coffee and went to sit in the window seat. *Dad will certainly ruin Christmas for all of us and Mom will just go along like she always does.* Staring out her window, Emma sat and thought for a while and after she finished her coffee.

She finally took a deep breath and told herself, *Fine, I'll write the letters, but I am writing them my way and if Dad doesn't like the idea, he can just wait until next year.*

It was mid-morning before Emma drove over to her parents' house. *If I am going to tackle this project,* Emma thought, *I will have to get an early start.* Knocking on her parent's front door softly, Emma stole a quick glance over to Sam's house, then turned around when her Mom answered the door.

"Emma, what are you doing here?" Ruth asked.

"Morning to you, too," Emma said. "I thought you would be up by now."

"I was just making myself a cup of coffee, want one?" Ruth asked as she made her way into the kitchen.

"No, I already had mine," Emma answered. "Everything okay here?"

"Well, we were at the hospital longer than we thought and by the time we got home both of us were exhausted," Ruth answered, sounding very tired. "Your Dad is still sleeping, so if you want to speak to him, you'll have to wait."

"Actually, I want to talk to you," Emma said. "I thought a lot about Dad last night and this morning and I have decided that since these letters mean so much to Dad that I will write them."

Surprised, Ruth took a seat on the couch in the living room, "Emma, I'm not sure that is a good idea."

"Mom, if I don't do this, you and I both know that Dad will be moping around here this holiday season and he will make you and the rest of us miserable," Emma said. "If I write them, then we are all happy."

"Do you have the time?" Ruth asked, knowing Emma's schedule.

"No, not really, but I will make the time," Emma promised. "Mom, when Dad and I were at the church, I offered myself and you to help him out, but now I know I have to do this."

Ruth sat and said nothing.

"Mom, what do you think?" Emma finally asked.

"I'm not sure if you should do this," Ruth said again.

"What's the problem?" Emma asked.

"Do you realize what you are taking on by doing this?" Ruth asked.

"Yes," Emma said confidently. "I'm writing letters for Christmas."

"There's more to it than just writing letters," Ruth explained.

"How many letters are we talking about anyway?" Emma asked her.

"Ten, according to your Dad" Ruth stated.

"Ten? That's it?" Emma asked, surprised.

"Yes, there are only ten this year," Ruth said seriously. "Emma, you have to understand each letter has purpose behind it. No two letters are the same. They all have a different story."

"Well, it would help if I knew the story behind each person I am writing to," Emma said.

"I do not know all of them, just some of them," Ruth shared.

"You and Dad talk about his Christmas letters?" Emma asked.

""Of course," her Mom smiled. "Why do you think I have supported him all these years?"

"Mom, you never told me," Emma said shaking her head.

"You never asked," Ruth reminded her. "I need to speak to your Dad about this first."

"Mom, I don't have time to wait. If I am going to write these letters and get them out on time, I am going to have to start today," Emma explained. "I promise I will make each one different."

Ruth stood up and paced her living room. Emma sat and let her mom process the idea through. Knowing how much these letters meant to her husband, Ruth gave in and gave Emma permission to write this year's Christmas letters.

"Do you want Dad's pen?" Ruth asked Emma.

"No, I have my own," Emma answered. "Besides, I don't want to take the chance of losing it. Do you have the addresses for these letters?"

"They are in your Dad's office, top drawer on the left right next to his journal," her Mom told her.

Emma made her way into her Dad's office and found his address book and journal. She also spotted the pen. She hesitated for a minute thinking about using it.

"No, I don't need it," she said firmly.

Shutting the drawer, Emma walked out with the journal and address book and headed for the door, "Please tell Dad I've got this. Don't worry, Mom. It will be alright."

"Emma," Ruth said as she gave her daughter a hug, "what you read in Dad's journal is private. You have to promise me that you will respect each person's story. As soon as you are finished reading it, bring that journal right back. Emma, sooner than later, okay?"

"Mom, I understand. I will not lose either one and I will write each letter with respect," Emma promised.

Opening the door, Emma turned to her Mom and said, "Tell you what, I will read it all tonight and I will bring back the journal first thing tomorrow."

That made Ruth smile, "Thank you, Emma. I would appreciate it and I know your Dad would, too."

Kissing her Mom, Emma told her, "I'll get them done before the holidays and we can all enjoy Thanksgiving and Christmas knowing Dad's mission has been fulfilled in spite of his broken arm."

She hugged her Mom, ran down to her car, and headed home.

Ruth stood in her doorway and thought, "I hope she knows what she is doing, and I pray I did the right thing."

Emma smiled as she turned up the radio. However, she knew she had to concentrate so she turned down the music. Driving back to her house, she decided she also needed to talk to Sam, but decided it would have to wait until tomorrow at school.

I'll swing by his office in the morning, she thought. By then all will be forgotten and hopefully forgiven.

When she reached her condo, she took off her jacket, made herself a cup of hot chocolate, and she sat down to look over her Dad's Christmas Letter address list. Her Dad had indicated which ones he had already written. Like her Mom had said, there were only ten names left on the list. Then she started to read her Dad's journal, but the more she read the more she felt like she was prying into their personal lives. Emma did not feel comfortable reading any further, so she closed the journal and set it down on the table next to the address list.

I can't do what Dad does. I do not know these people like he does, she thought.

Emma picked up her phone and called her Mom.

"Hi, Mom. Look, I can't use Dad's journal. I started reading it and I felt like I was invading these people's privacy," Emma told her. "So, I will bring the journal back to you later this afternoon if that is okay."

When her Mom did not immediately respond, Emma asked, "Mom, are you there?"

"Yes, sorry, Emma," Ruth said slowly. "I'm relieved, but what are you going to do about the letters then?"

Taking a deep breath, "If I am going to write these letters, then they are going to have to be my Christmas Letters."

"Emma, I'm proud of you," Ruth said. "Thank you."

"I haven't done anything yet," Emma said, wondering how this was all going to play out.

"I know, but you will," Ruth said knowingly. "Come for dinner tonight and we'll talk."

"Okay," Emma agreed.

Hanging up the phone, she thought about what she had said.

My Christmas Letters, she said to herself and got a strange tug in her stomach. *I do not know if I can do this.*

Taking another deep breath, Emma threw back her shoulders, looked up, and said, "I can do this, but I need Your help!"

Emma sat down at her desk and started to write her first Christmas Letter. A couple of hours later, Emma had finished two letters.

Not bad, she told herself as she got up to stretch.

Just then, her doorbell rang. *I wonder who that could be,* Emma thought as she got up and opened her door.

Sam was standing in her doorway holding a dozen yellow roses.

"What are you doing here?" Emma said rather rudely.

"Emma, please, we need to talk," Sam said.

"I'm busy right now," Emma said starting to close the door.

"Please, can I come in?" Sam pleaded softly.

"Only for a minute, I have a lot to do today," Emma told him. "I'm going to...,"

"I know," Sam interrupted her, "I just got off the phone with your Mom and she told me what you're doing for your Dad."

"You called my Mom?" Emma asked.

"I saw your car at your parents' house this morning and when you left so quickly I got worried, so I called to make sure you and your Dad were alright," Sam explained.

"We are both fine and I really do have a lot to do," Emma said, really not wanting to get into another discussion with Sam about the Christmas Letters.

"Emma, I came to say I'm sorry about last night," Sam apologized and handed her the flowers. "And to say you're doing the right thing helping your Dad like this."

"I'm glad you think so," Emma said. "Thank you for the flowers."

"Is there anything I can do?" Sam asked.

"No" Emma answered. "With all due respect, these people have entrusted my Dad with their stories and it isn't anybody else's business."

"You are right," Sam agreed. "These letters and who they go to are none of my business. I will go and leave you to your letters."

As Sam was walking toward the door, he noticed the labels by her computer and asked, "What are these for?"

"If you must know, they're for Dad," Emma told him.

"You are going to use labels on the Christmas Letters?" Sam asked. "But your Dad always wrote out the addresses by hand. You are not writing the letters on the computer, are you? Emma, you're not doing this for the right reason if you think you can mass produce these letters."

Angry, Emma declared, "Sam, this is none of your business. How do you know how my Dad writes and addresses his letters anyway?"

"He told me," Sam told her.

"Really?" she asked. "When?"

"Halloween night," Sam said, realizing this was angering her even further for some reason.

"Well, I am telling you, you're not family so you have no right to lecture me about my family. From now on I would appreciate it if you would mind your own business. Now get out!"

Emma opened the door and then slammed it as soon as Sam stepped out of the doorway.

Chapter 9

Who does he think he is, Emma thought as she paced the floor, too angry to concentrate on writing another Christmas Letter. *I am writing these letters for Dad and each one will be different, so why is Sam lecturing me? He has no right.*

Trying to calm herself down, she sat down at her desk and stared at the blank piece of paper in front of her. She tried to write something cheerful for the person who was receiving this particular letter when a soft knock came from her door.

*It better not be **him**,* Emma thought as she jumped up and looked through the peep hole.

"Go away, Sam," she told him.

"Emma," Sam said, "open the door, please."

Emma stood there for a moment, then opened the door slightly, "What do **you** want?"

"Can I come in?" he asked quietly.

"No!" she answered pointedly.

"I'm sorry, you're right its none of my business and I overstepped. I apologize," Sam said quickly before she could close the door in his face. "This is your business and I promise to keep my mouth shut. If there is anything I can do, let me know. I would like to help."

Opening the door, a little wider, she threatened, "If you make one comment or criticism, you are out."

"I promise, not a word," Sam said raising his right hand as a pledge.

"Okay, come in," she said and opened just door wide enough for him to come in.

Shutting the door, Emma took Sam's coat and laid it on the couch.

Then she stood right in front of him and said, "Don't you ever speak to me that way again!"

"I won't. I am sorry," Sam said sincerely.

"By the way, the next time you open your mouth to tell me I am doing something the wrong way, you might want to make sure you know what you are talking about," Emma said tossing him her Dad's address book.

"These labels will be used by Dad when and if he wants to. I was planning on entering all the names and addresses my Dad has in his book into the computer. That way, if he needs to send another letter or note he has the address at his disposal. I thought it would be easier especially if someone moved. All he has to do is change it on the computer list."

"That's a really good idea," Sam agreed.

"So, if you want to help, sit down in front of my computer and start entering all the names and addresses from his book," Emma said as she went over to the table to work on another Christmas Letter.

"I can do that," Sam said as he sat down and looked at the address book. "WOW! This is going to take days!"

"I know, but when it's finished, Dad will have his address book at his fingertips and he can reach out to whomever he pleases," Emma explained.

"What made you think of doing this?" Sam asked as he started typing in the names in the book.

"Mom has her list on the computer, so when she writes our Christmas cards, she uses Christmas labels," Emma explained. "With her busy schedule, that is the only way our Christmas cards get done on time."

As time passed, Sam kept his word and said no more about how Emma was handling the task of writing the letters for her Dad.

When she was finished with the third letter, Emma said, "I don't understand why some people get a card and a letter from our family."

Not saying a word, Sam continued to enter names and addresses into the computer.

"Sam, did you hear me?" Emma asked.

"I'm sorry, I did not know if you were talking to me and wanting an answer," Sam said cautiously. "I don't know, but I am sure your Dad has a good reason for why he does what he does. Maybe you should ask him and not me?"

When Emma was finished with the fourth letter, she stopped and could not believe what time it was and how much her hand was starting to cramp.

"Are you alright?" Sam asked.

"I'm fine," she said. "My hand is cramping up, though. I can't believe Dad writes these all out by hand. No wonder it takes him so long."

"Why don't we take a break and go get some lunch?" Sam suggested.

Emma agreed. She needed time to recharge and the best way was to eat. Emma grabbed her Dad's journal, her purse, and her coat.

"What are you doing with the journal?" Sam asked as he grabbed his coat.

"I'm returning it," Emma explained. "When we are finished with lunch, I am going to stop by my parents' house, so you might as well take your car. You have helped me out enough for today."

"Are you sure?" Sam asked.

"I'm sure and thank you, it looks like you made headway with the addresses," Emma said with a smile.

"I don't know about that," Sam said, grateful she was no longer angry with him. "I marked the page where I left off."

"Great! I'll meet you at the diner," Emma said as she locked the door behind them.

When they got to the diner, it seemed a little crowded, but they managed to grab a table in the very back.

"Hi, Sam! What are you two up to today?" the waitress asked.

"Hi, Heather, we were discussing the annual Christmas lunch for the staff," Sam said.

Emma smiled, "Can we get two bowls of chili and I would like a water with lemon."

"Sam, do you want your usual, a coke?" the waitress asked.

"Yes, thank you," Sam answered with a smile.

"Coming right up," Heather smiled and walked away.

"How did she know who you were?" Emma asked Sam.

"I come here every morning and have breakfast," Sam explained.

"You do?" Emma asked, surprised.

"I do," Sam admitted. "They have the best oatmeal I have ever tasted."

"Why did you tell her we were talking about the Christmas luncheon?" Emma asked.

"Because I was going to speak to you about it earlier today, but I almost forgot," Sam told her. "Are you still organizing it?"

"I am, why?" Emma asked.

"I was just wondering if you are sure you can still do it with everything you have on your plate now," Sam said.

"I'm sure," Emma told him. "It really isn't difficult. Everybody pitches in and helps."

"Here's your water with lemon and a coke for you, Sam," the waitress said. "Your chili will be out soon."

"Thanks, Heather," Sam smiled.

"Okay, then what can I do to help with the luncheon?" Sam asked Emma.

"Since you're the teacher's favorite baker, would you mind baking cookies?" Emma asked.

"Sure, how many cookies do you want?" Sam asked.

Hesitating, as she calculated quickly in her head, Emma said, "I guess enough for about a fifty people."

"That's a lot of cookies," Sam said laughing.

"Yes, but I am sure you are up to the challenge," Emma smiled. "Think of it this way, the teachers will owe you big time."

Picking up his glass, Sam said, "Then you have a deal."

Once Heather brought their chili, Sam noticed that Emma was quiet, "Are you alright?"

"I'm fine, but a bit overwhelmed," Emma admitted.

"Emma, I'm sorry for the way I spoke to earlier, I had no right," Sam said sincerely. "You didn't deserve that."

"I can see now that you only had my Dad's best interest at heart. I do, too. I promised Mom this morning that I will write these letters respectfully," Emma told Sam. "Mom reminded me that each person has a story, so I need to keep reminding myself of that."

"When I first met your parents," Sam told her. "Your Dad and I talked a while in his office."

"I remember," Emma smiled. "You two were in there a long time."

"We talked about a lot of things," Sam explained. "He spoke to me about his writings, too. That's why I thought about giving him the pen."

Intrigued, Emma sat back and paid attention, "What did he say?"

"He told me about a letter he wrote many years ago," Sam said. "It was a Christmas letter and how much the letter meant to the people who received it."

"He shared with you someone's story?" Emma asked.

"Not exactly," Sam said. "He just told me that many years ago, he knew that he had to write a letter to this particular person and that receiving the letter meant a lot to that person. He also told me that writing the letters is not about him, but he truly believes that he is doing what God has called him to do."

"I have asked him about his letters before and he has never shared anything," Emma told Sam sadly.

Sam looked at her carefully and said, "I can only tell you that before your Dad sits down and writes a letter, he spends many hours talking to the one who is about to receive a letter. He just doesn't sit down and write whatever comes to mind."

"Neither do I!" Emma said defensively. "These letters are not just from me, they represent Dad, so they have to be what I believe he would write to them."

"How do you know what to write if you don't have a story behind it?" Sam asked.

"I wondered that myself after I decided not to use Dad's journal," Emma told him. "So, I am praying that God gives me the words for each person and I'm writing what comes to my heart."

As Emma and Sam finished their lunch, neither one spoke any more about the letters. Instead, they spoke about the upcoming Thanksgiving holiday and school break.

"When do your parents get in?" Emma asked.

"Tomorrow," Sam answered. "I'm going home now to get my house in order."

"I'm looking forward to meeting them," Emma said with a smile.

"They are looking forward to meeting you, too," Sam told her.

After lunch, Emma followed Sam home and pulled into her parents' driveway.

Grabbing the journal, Emma walked in the front door, softly calling out, "Hello?"

"Emma," her mom said. "I wasn't expecting you so early."

"Sam and I took a break and had lunch at the café," Emma explained. "I decided that I would stop by and give Dad back his journal. How is he by the way?"

"He's resting. How's it going?" Ruth asked curiously.

"Don't worry, Mom, I've got this," Emma said with a smile.

"You've got what?" her Dad asked as he walked into the kitchen.

"I thought you were resting," Ruth said.

"I was," Frank said. "But I heard Emma come in."

"The letters," Emma said, answering her dad's question. "Didn't Mom tell you?"

"I haven't had a chance," Ruth said.

"What are you two talking about?" Frank asked.

"Emma has decided that she is going to write the rest of the Christmas Letters for you," Ruth explained.

"No, she can't," Frank said. "She knows nothing about these people."

"That's true," Ruth agreed, but before she could explain, Frank noticed the journal in Emma's hands.

"What are you doing with my journal, Emma?" he demanded. "My journal is private, and you have no right to be reading it!"

"Frank, stop!" Ruth said, raising her voice.

"Ruth, she has no right," Frank exclaimed, raising his voice as well.

"Can I talk?" Emma asked before the conversation escalated any further. "Please, Dad, sit down."

"I don't want to sit down," Frank said angrily.

"Frank, sit!" Ruth said firmly.

Frank grudgingly sat at the counter.

"Early this morning I came over here to tell you that I wanted to write the Christmas Letters. You were still sleeping, so Mom and I talked. I asked for the journal and your address book, which I still have by the way. Mom didn't feel right about me taking the journal, but I insisted that I needed to understand these people's stories, so I took the journal."

Frank was about to speak, but Emma continued, "Dad, I was wrong. When I got home, I started reading your journal and I just couldn't. I called Mom and I told her that I was going to bring your journal back this afternoon, so here it is. What these people have told you is private and I had no right reading it."

Reaching for his journal, Frank said, "Thank you, Emma."

"You're welcome," Emma answered.

"How are you going to write the Letters if you have no idea what to write?" her Dad asked her.

"Well, I am putting that into God's hands," Emma told him. "I am praying that He will give me the words as I write each letter."

"This is not a good idea," Frank said as he rose and walked around the kitchen.

"I promise that each letter will be appropriate," Emma told him, surprised at his response.

"How are you going to get them all done in time?" he asked her. "You have told us numerous times that you are so busy."

"I'll figure it out," Emma assured him. "Besides, four are already written."

"Emma, it takes me days to write one," her Dad said in amazement. "This is wrong, I don't like it."

Frank left the kitchen and went to sit in his favorite chair.

Emma walked into the living room and sat across from her Dad, "Dad, I can do this."

"I know you can, but you are doing it all wrong," he said shaking his head. "Are you using my pen?"

"No, I have my own pens," Emma answered.

"Do you still have my address book?" her Dad asked realizing she had only returned his journal.

"Sam is putting all of the addresses into the computer," Emma told him.

"Why would he do that?" Frank asked her.

"So, it will be easier for you in the future," Emma explained.

"Well, I don't want them in the computer," Frank complained.

"Sam started it and I will be finishing up this week, so you can have all your addresses and your book back at the end of next week," Emma said standing up to leave.

"Why is Sam involved?" Frank asked starting to yell.

"He wanted to help you, too," Emma answered, realizing she was starting to yell as well.

"Emma, this is not the way I write them," her dad complained. "I never use the computer and I definitely never use labels."

"I am not using labels or the computer for your letters," she yelled, shaking her head.

"You are not writing the letters this year either," her Dad said firmly.

"I thought you would be happy and appreciate that they would still be written even though you have broken your arm," Emma said, confused by her Dad's attitude. "Not only are you not appreciative, you sound bitter. What's really going on?"

Frank refused to answer, going off into his bedroom.

"Mom, what is Dad's problem?" Emma asked, confused by the way the conversation had gone.

"I don't know, but I will find out," Ruth told her. "I'm going to let him cool off first, though. Does Sam know who you are writing to?"

"No, but he's being quite annoying," Emma told her mother.

"Tell me what happened," Ruth said walking over and sitting down by Emma on the sofa.

"Well, Sam came over this morning to apologize for speaking to me harshly last night," Emma explained. "It's okay now, but I let him know that he better not ever speak to me that way again."

"My, what did he say to get you so upset?" Ruth asked.

"It's not important, but this morning he brought flowers to apologize and spotted the labels. Just like Dad, he assumed that I was going to write the letters on the computer and use labels on the envelopes," Emma said shaking her head. "What is with them always assuming anyways?"

"I don't know," Ruth admitted.

"I can't count how many times you told Ben and me that we should never assume anything," Emma said in her best imitation of her mother's voice. "Make sure you have all of the facts."

Tapping her daughter's hand, Ruth smiled and said, "I'm glad you remember."

"How can I forget? It seemed like you were telling me that every day," Emma laughed.

"At times, I did," Ruth admitted. "But as you got older, you figured life out for yourself."

"Mom," Emma asked. "What do you think is going on with Dad?"

"I think I know, but I am not going to assume," her Mom said with a smile. "I am going to find out for sure and then I will let you know."

"I have never seen Dad so angry," Emma said with a shiver.

"You are right about that," Ruth agreed. "He is certainly angry about something, but I don't think it's you. I think it is something else, but like I said, I'll let you know."

"So, back to you and Sam," Ruth said, redirecting the conversation. "Sam assumed about the labels and the letters and then what?"

"Well, I snapped and told him to get out. He left, but then he came back. We both calmed down and then I explained what I was doing and why I was doing it." Emma took a breath. "He wanted to help, so I put him to work adding names and addresses Dad has in his book to the computer list so whenever Dad wants to reach out, he can."

"That's a good idea," Ruth said. "I use labels for my Christmas cards."

"I know, that is where I got the idea," Emma said smiling at her Mom. "I really thought Dad would appreciate it, but now I'm not sure. He was so angry!"

"You let me worry about that, but now I think you should head home and get some rest," Ruth suggested. "I am going to go speak to your Dad and see if I can get to the bottom of this."

Getting up off the couch, Emma kissed her Mom, grabbed her coat, and made her way down to her car. *I hope Dad doesn't take out his anger on Mom*, she thought as she pulled out the driveway.

Emma shook her head and smiled. *If Dad thinks he is going to get away with the way he treated me and yelled at Mom, he better think twice.* She knew her Mom would be setting her Dad straight! His broken arm would not be a viable excuse for such behavior!

Chapter 10

Ruth watched Emma back out of her driveway. Then she made her way to her bedroom where she found Frank sitting is the recliner staring out the window.

"If you are done staring out the window, would you please tell me why you yelled at my daughter?" Ruth said.

"I thought she was ours," Frank grumbled.

"Not when you treat her like that she's not," Ruth said firmly. "Frank, she did not deserve that and you know it. Now, what's going on?"

"Nothing," Frank mumbled.

"I'm waiting," Ruth declared, sitting on their bed. "Frank!"

Turning around, Frank faced his wife, "These letters belong to me and she has no right to write them. I know their stories, Emma does not."

"Emma is just trying to help," Ruth explained patiently.

"That is not how I do things, Ruth, and you know it," he said stubbornly.

"I do, but you can't write, so we have to trust Emma's judgement on this," Ruth challenged him. "Frank, do you trust Emma?"

Silence was his answer, so she stared at him.

"I do," Frank finally answered. "I'm just use to doing it my way."

"Well, this year it's her way," Ruth said decisively. "Emma was right. Just because she is not writing the way you do doesn't mean that she is doing it wrong. Next year you can write them whatever way you want."

Getting up, Ruth kissed her husband and went back into the living room.

Staring out the window again, Frank grumbled, "To me she is."

He looked up into heaven and added, "She's doing it all wrong, they were **my** letters."

Ruth came back into the room and asked, "What did you say?"

"I said she is doing it wrong!" Frank said stubbornly.

"Says who? You?" Ruth challenged him.

"Yes, **me**!" he said angrily.

"Frank, I have been very patient with you since you broke your arm, but Emma is right, you sound bitter and you are starting to take it out on me," Ruth declared firmly. "I don't like it or deserve it!"

"Ruth, I'm sorry," Frank apologized. "You're right. I am angry, but it's not at Emma or you."

"Then who are you angry at?" Ruth asked him.

"I'm mad at God," Frank said shaking his head.

Shocked, Ruth asked, "Frank, why are you mad at God?"

"Ruth, please leave me be," Frank pleaded miserably. "I need to figure this out myself."

"Alright, but I will need an explanation from you when you are ready," Ruth told him.

"I know," he said as he got up and went to his office.

Ruth knew what she needed to do, but she was too angry to pursue the conversation any further, so she just left the room.

For the rest of the day, Frank stayed in his office.

As she prepared for bed, Ruth knocked on the office door and asked, "Frank, are you coming to bed?"

"In a little while," he responded.

Ruth hesitated, pushed open the door, and walked over to her husband.

Grabbing his face and with tears in her eyes, she said gently, "I know you are hurting and I wish you would tell me what's bothering you. I love you."

She kissed him and walked out.

The next day, Emma made her way down to the nurse's station at lunch time to find her Mom taking the temperature of a first grader.

"Hi," Ruth greeted her.

"Jennifer told me that you were here, but I couldn't believe it," Emma said. "I thought you were staying home and taking care of Dad."

"He told me to go and besides he's just watching TV," Ruth told her. "I'm leaving in a few minutes to go check on him and bring him lunch."

"Guess that means I'm on own my own for lunch today," Emma smiled.

"Yes, sorry, I have to go," Ruth said picking up her purse. "I'll call you later and let you know how's he's doing."

"Mom," Emma asked, "Did you get a chance to talk to Dad?"

Not wanting to alarm her daughter, "I did, but I can't talk about that now. I have to go. I will talk to you later, okay?"

Walking back to her classroom, Emma was surprised to see Josh coming towards her, "Josh, I thought you were going to try to not come down here for the entire week."

"I'm not sick, Ms. Emma, I am supposed to tell you that Mr. Sam is looking for you," Josh told her very seriously.

"Thanks, Josh, you are a good messenger," Emma smiled at him. "You can go to recess."

Emma made her way down to Sam's office where he was eating his lunch behind his desk.

"Hi, Josh said you wanted to see me?" she asked him.

"Yes, care to join me for lunch?" Sam asked pointing to all the food displayed on his desk.

"Where did you get all of this food?" Emma asked.

"My Mom," Sam laughed.

"I thought your parents were not coming in until tonight," Emma said, pulling up a chair on the other side of his desk.

"They got an earlier flight and came in last night," Sam explained. "It's a good thing I went home after lunch yesterday or my house would not have been in order for my Mother."

"Does she approve of your house and all of the Christmas decorating we did?" Emma asked.

"Mother is very pleased and so was Father," Sam said nodding his head. "And Mother made enough food last night to feed an army."

"It smells wonderful," Emma said hungrily.

"It's lasagna," Sam said as he handed her a plate. "Did you get a chance to enter any more addresses?"

"Taking a mouth full of lasagna," Emma shook her head and wiped her mouth. "No, and I'm not sure I will."

"Why not?" Sam asked. "I thought you wanted to get all of the addresses in this week for your Dad."

"I did until I spoke to him yesterday," Emma said sadly.

"What happened yesterday?" Sam asked knowing how hard Emma had worked on her dad's Christmas Letters yesterday.

"Dad pretty much bit my head off for writing the letters and putting the addresses into the computer," Emma explained trying to stay in control of her emotions.

"That doesn't sound like your Dad," Sam commented.

"I know," Emma agreed. "He was very angry, almost bitter."

"That definitely does not sound like Frank at all!" Sam said, looking at her to see how she was handling it.

"No, it doesn't," Emma said shaking her head. "He even snapped at Mom. She told me she was going to find out why, but I haven't heard anything yet. She just left to go take him some lunch."

"Well, maybe tonight you will find out something," Sam suggested.

"I hope so," Emma said. "I have never seen my Dad furious like he was yesterday."

When Ruth pulled into her driveway, she sat in her car preparing herself for whatever she was going to walk in to. Making her way up the stairs, she opened the front door to find Frank sitting in front of the TV watching the noon news.

"Hi, I brought you lunch," she said in a cheery voice.

"I'm not hungry," Frank mumbled.

"Frank, you have to eat," Ruth told him.

"I'll eat later," he told her, but she was not convinced he really meant it.

Going into the living room, Ruth looked at Frank and said, "So, what's going on?"

"I told you yesterday," Frank said impatiently.

"I know what you told me, and you also told me you would explain," Ruth declared. "I am ready for an explanation."

"Ruth, I can't talk about this right now," he said and got up to go to his office.

"How long are you going to stay mad at God?" she yelled after him.

Saying nothing, he just went in and shut the door.

"How long until You move or move him?" she asked looking up to heaven.

Looking out, she could see two people trying to get into Sam's house. Grabbing her coat, Ruth went outside and crossed the street.

"Hi, can I help you?" Ruth asked the woman.

"I certainly hope so. My son lives here and my husband left the key on the kitchen table, so now we have no way to get in," the woman explained.

Reaching out to shake the woman's hand, Ruth said, "I know your son, Sam. My daughter and I work at the same school. My name is Ruth Trask."

"Hello, it's nice to meet you," the woman responded. "I'm Mary Watson and that man walking around the house is Sam's father, James."

"It's nice to meet you," Ruth said. "I have a key at my house. Sam gave it to me thinking that maybe you might need it."

Both women laughed.

"Sam knows his father," Mary said with a smile.

"I'll be right back," Ruth said, then turned around and suggested, "On second thought, why don't you follow me home and I can introduce you to my husband."

"Don't you need to get back to school?" Mary asked.

"No, not today," Ruth explained. "My husband broke his arm and I came home to check on him. I called my daughter and told her to tell the school principal that I was not coming back today."

"I'm sorry to hear about your husband," Mary said sympathetically. "How did he break his arm?"

"He fell on a patch of ice at the church Saturday," Ruth said.

They both turned around as they heard footsteps coming up behind them.

"Hi, I'm James," the man said.

"I'm Ruth, come on in," she invited them as they got to her front door. "I will go get Frank."

"Ruth, you have a beautiful home," Mary said looking around.

"Thank you," Ruth responded. "I'll be right back."

Ruth peeked into the office, but Frank was not there, so she went to their bedroom to find him staring out the window again.

Closing the door behind her, she said, "Frank, you need to come out and meet Sam's parents."

"What are they doing here?" Frank asked irritably.

"They locked themselves out, so I came to get the key Sam gave me," Ruth explained.

"Tell them I'm sick," Frank told her without getting up out of his chair.

"Frank Trask, get up!" Ruth told him, disgusted with his antics.

"Ruth, I'm in no mood to talk to anybody," Frank told her.

Walking over to her husband, Ruth said, "Frank, look at me, I don't know what your problem is and right now I don't care. What I do care about is how you act right now for your wife's and daughter's boss."

"Jennifer is your boss, not Sam!" Frank said rebelliously.

"Fine, I give up," Ruth said shaking her head sadly. "You stay here and feel sorry for yourself. You might be mad at God, but you don't have to take it out on the rest of us. By the way, you might want to stop and think about how **He** feels about your behavior right now!"

Ruth walked out and approached her guests wondering if they heard any of that.

"I'm sorry, my husband is not feeling well, so you'll have to meet him some other time," Ruth told them, handing them the key.

"That's okay, thanks for the key," Mary said, then she and James walked back over to Sam's house.

As Ruth watched them leave, tears fell down her cheeks.

"Did they leave?" Frank called to her from the bedroom door.

"What do you think?" Ruth said angrily, then she got up and grabbed her coat.

"Where are you going?" Frank asked.

"School," Ruth told him. "You certainly don't need me, so I might as well go back to work or do you have something to tell me?"

Frank shook his head.

"Fine!" Ruth and left Frank standing there with his mouth open.

It was the first time in forty years she left and did not kiss her husband goodbye.

While Emma and Sam finished their lunch, Emma noticed her Mom's car pulling back into the school parking lot.

"Mom's here," Emma said, wondering what was going on.

"I thought you said she wasn't coming back?" Sam said, looking out at the parking lot as well.

"That is what she said when she called a little while ago," Emma said. "I think I need to go and see if everything is alright. Thanks for lunch, Sam."

When Emma met her Mom at the door, she could tell that something was wrong.

"Mom, is everything alright?" Emma asked her.

"It's your Dad, but I don't want to talk about it," Ruth told her, obviously upset. "I'm going back to work."

I wonder what happened, Emma thought.

As she walked back to her classroom, her phone rang.

"Hi, Dad," Emma said. "Mom? Yes, she's here. Okay, I'll tell her."

"Tell who what?" asked Jennifer walking up beside her friend.

"Jenn, something is going on with my parents and I'm scared. I have never seemed them so angry," Emma said worriedly.

"Come see me after school and we'll talk," Jennifer told her. "Now, I hate to pull rank, but you need to hurry and get to class."

They both smiled and Emma hugged her friend. Then Emma walked swiftly back to her classroom.

How slow can an afternoon go, Emma thought as she finished up her day. As soon as she wrapped everything up in her classroom, she turned off the light and headed to Jennifer's office. Since she had not heard from her Mom and Jennifer was not in her office, Emma decided to give her Mom a call.

Jennifer walked in just then and sat behind her desk.

"Mom's phone went straight to voice mail," Emma said as she sat down across from Jennifer.

"Emma, what is going on?" Jennifer asked. "You and your Mom have had the same look on your faces all afternoon."

"I don't know where to start," Emma said as the tears she'd held in check all day began to fall.

Grabbing a tissue box and handing it to Emma, Jennifer said, "Take a breath and start from the beginning."

"Well, you know Dad fell Saturday and broke his arm," Emma began.

"Yes," Jennifer nodded.

"It was his right arm, his writing arm," Emma said, shaking her head sadly.

"I didn't know that," Jennifer said sitting straight up in her chair.

"So, I decided that I would write the Christmas Letters for Dad since he can't," Emma explained. "When I told him, instead of being happy about it, he felt betrayed and angry."

"What did your mom say?" Jennifer asked.

"She was all for it," Emma told her. "We both knew that Dad would be moping around the house because his letters would not be going out this year. I thought if I wrote them then Dad would be happy."

Emma shook her head sadly, "Jenn, I have never seen Dad like this. He screamed at me! I am starting to think that maybe he did hit his head when he fell."

"The hospital checked him out, didn't they?" Jennifer asked.

"Yes, his head was fine," Emma said as she got up and started pacing around the office. "Mom and I can't figure out why he is so angry."

"Have you asked him?" Jennifer asked.

"He won't even talk to me," Emma explained. "Mom said she thinks she knows, but doesn't want to say anything until she finds out from Dad. I don't know what else to do. I'm worried about both of them!"

"Oh, I almost forgot," Emma added. "You know how Mom uses labels for her Christmas cards?"

"Yes, of course," Jennifer nodded.

"Well, I thought it would be a good idea for me to input all of the addresses Dad has in his address book into the computer as I was working on his letters. That way, if someone moves or if he wants to write a letter or a note to someone, it's all right there at his fingertips."

"That's a great idea, Emma!" Jennifer smiled. "If you enter the addresses that I have, I will be forever in your debt."

Laughing, Emma shook her head, "Not right now, but I will keep that in mind."

"But seriously, Jenn, what am I going to do?" Emma asked her friend.

"Emma, it seems to me you have two options," Jennifer suggested. "You can continue to write them without your dad's blessing or you can quit."

"I don't care about the letters as much as I do about what this is doing to Mom and Dad," Emma said sadly.

"Well, if it were me, I would start by praying for them," Jennifer suggested thoughtfully.

"Good idea!" Emma said with a smile. "You're the best!"

As Emma made her way to her car, she saw Sam and flagged him down.

Rolling down her window, she said, "I'm heading over to Mom's to see how they are doing."

"Are you okay?" Sam asked.

"I'll let you know after I talk to Mom and hopefully Dad," Emma promised.

She rolled up her window and made her way to her parents' home turning up her radio. Then she did as Jennifer had suggested and asked God to touch her parents.

Chapter 11

As Emma drove, she listened to a Christmas song she had heard many times, but this time something started to stir in her heart and she smiled. As Emma pulled into her parents' driveway, she sat and listened to the rest of the song. She began to hum the song under her breath as she collected her thoughts and made her way to up to the front door.

"Hi," she said as she took off her coat and hung it on the coat rack.

"In here," yelled her Dad sitting in his favorite chair.

"What are **you** doing here," he shot at her.

"I'm fine, Dad, thanks for asking," Emma said, refusing to take the bait.

"Sorry," her Dad said, not looking at her, just staring at the TV. "What are you doing here?"

"Dad, we need to talk," Emma said gently, but firmly.

"We already did," Frank said, still refusing to look at her.

"Yes, we did," Emma admitted. "But I don't like the way we left things."

That got her Dad's attention long enough for her to grab the remote out of his hand and turn off the TV.

"I really need you to listen to me for a minute," Emma began.

"What is going on in here?" Ruth asked as she walked into the room.

"I am trying to talk to Dad," Emma explained, "but he's being rude."

"Frank, are you going to tell her, or am I?" her Mom asked him.

"It's none of her business," her Dad said stubbornly.

"Okay," Ruth threatened. "If you are going to be rude, I'll tell her right now."

"Alright, I will listen to Emma," her Dad said. "Emma, you have my attention."

"I have been thinking about the Letters," Emma began.

Frank rolled his eyes, "Dad, just hear me out. I should not have assumed that you would want me to write the Letters for you this year. I should have asked first. I am sorry."

Frank could not believe what his daughter was saying.

"So, as I see it, we can do this, one of two ways," Emma said, having Frank's full attention now. "You give me your blessing and support, and I will write the Letters. Or, no more Letters go out and you explain to whomever is receiving the rest that this year they will receive a phone call from you instead. It's up to you."

"You mean you'll stop writing them?" her Dad asked.

"I do," Emma agreed.

"You will not send out the letters if I don't want you to?" he asked.

"That is exactly what I am saying," Emma told him. "However, I have to tell you, four letters went out already, so you only have to make six calls."

Frank stood, walked over to the window, and smiled.

"Emma, I appreciate you coming over and I am sorry for my behavior," he said. "I have said over and over this is my project not yours or your Mom's."

"So, what do you want to do?" Emma asked him.

"I want to make the calls," Frank said firmly.

"Oh, okay," Emma said looking at her Mom.

"Now, I have to think about how I can do this," he said and went into his office.

"Well, I guess that's that," Emma said, shaking her head. "Mom, I have to admit, I can't believe it. I'm a little disappointed, but I guess I should not be surprised. As Dad has said so many times, this is his project."

"Yes, but I am starting to wonder if your Dad is doing this for the right reason," Ruth admitted.

"I don't know, but now that it has been settled, I have to go," Emma said.

"You should take a few minutes and go over to Sam's. His parents are in town and I know they would like to meet you," Ruth told Emma. "They're nice people. I met them earlier."

"Oh, really? How?" Emma asked wondering how Mom had managed to meet them before she did.

"I'll let Sam explain it to you. Tell Mary and James I said hello," hugging her daughter. "You better go. I will see you tomorrow."

"Mom, are you alright?" Emma asked, wondering if her Mom was as confused as she was by her Dad's response.

"I'm fine now go," Ruth said, pushing her daughter out the door.

Opening the office door, she asked Frank, "What are you doing?"

"Looking for my address book," Frank answered.

"Emma has it," Ruth reminded him. "She told you that earlier."

"Well, I need Emma to bring it back as soon as possible," Frank said. "I need to start making these calls right away."

"Emma just went to Sam's, so I will call her later," Ruth told him. "She can bring it by tomorrow."

"No, I need it today," he snapped.

"Frank, I said you will get it tomorrow," Ruth promised.

"Fine, but make sure she gets to me," Frank said grudgingly. "I want to start calling these people and explain the situation."

"Explain what situation, exactly, Frank?" Ruth asked pointedly. "Explain that you're mad at God or why you are acting like a spoiled child?"

Closing the door, he yelled, "I'm not mad anymore."

Ruth did not smile. Without saying a word, Ruth made her way out of her husband's office and went into her bedroom where she kept her Bible and her journal. In no time, she had filled up an entire page and a half in her journal. When she was finished, she closed her journal and sat where her husband had sat earlier and stared out the window with tears filling her eyes. Then she took a breath and smiled knowing God was going to work this all out.

"Hi," Emma said when Sam answered his door. "Mom said I should stop over and meet your parents."

"Come in," he said as he took her coat. "Mother, Father this is Emma Trask."

"Hi," Emma said, reaching out her hand.

"It's nice to meet you, Emma," Sam's Mom said warmly. "I'm Mary Watson, I met your mom earlier today. In fact, she saved us."

"Oh, really? How?" Emma asked.

"Hi Emma, I'm James Watson," Sam's Dad said, "I accidently locked us out of Sam's house earlier and your mom had a key and let us back in."

"I must say, you look a lot like your mom," Sam's Mom said with a smile.

"I will take that as a compliment," Emma responded.

"You should, she beautiful inside and out," Mary said sincerely.

"How is your Dad feeling?" James asked.

"He's happier now, I think," Emma told her.

"Dinner is ready, Emma will you join us?" Mary asked, directing them all into the dining room.

"Thank you, I would love to," Emma replied. "Wow! The table looks beautiful."

"Oh, thank you. I didn't do much," Mary said, but Emma could tell that Mary had carefully lined up all the glasses and silverware to set a perfect table.

Grabbing hands, James led them in prayer.

"Emma, what did you mean your Dad is happier now?" Mary asked. "Your Mom said he had broken his arm in a fall and wasn't feeling well earlier."

Taking a sip of water from a crystal glass, Emma replied, "Yes, he did. In fact, it was his right arm which is now preventing him from writing what he calls his Christmas Letters. He was very upset about that, so I went over to Mom and Dad's and offered to write those letters for him."

"That was nice of you, Emma," Mary said as she passed her a plate of meat.

"Well, I am afraid I handled this whole writing thing poorly as my Dad got angry and upset," Emma said as she took a slice of meat and passed the plate to Sam. "This looks delicious, Mary!"

"Thank you," Mary smiled. "You were saying about these letters your Dad writes?"

"Well, as we talked more about it, I suggested I could write the letters for him or maybe he could call the people on his list this year instead," Emma explained.

"What did Frank decide?" Sam asked, knowing how much drama had already surrounded the letter writing situation.

"Dad chose to make phone calls," Emma answered. "At first, I was surprised but now I get it. It is his project. So, that's one less thing I have on my plate."

"I'm sorry to hear that your Dad took that fall," Mary said. "James, does that remind you of anything?"

Shaking his head, James answered, "It does, but do we really need to get into that?"

"Father, forgot to put sand on our steps leading up to the front door," Sam said. "He fell and broke his leg."

"I am so sorry, James," Emma said.

"I told him repeatedly that someone was going to fall and he didn't listen," Mary said shaking her head. "But Emma, I can tell you after that James made sure he put sand down every time it snowed, even if it was only a half an inch."

Turning to her son she said, "That reminds me, Sam, we are going to need to buy some sand tomorrow. I am sure between now and Christmas, we will need it."

"Oh, that reminds me, Sam, I won't be needing your help with entering the addresses anymore," Emma said. "Dad made it very clear he doesn't want us to do it."

"I'm sorry to hear that," Sam said, knowing that must have been another disappointment for Emma.

"What kind of letters does your Dad write?" James asked.

"My Dad picks certain people from town which he believes need a special Christmas Letter. Each year from November first until Christmas, my family does not see my Dad much as he writes these special letters out by hand."

"WOW! That's a long time to be without your family and a lot of time writing," Mary said.

"I know, I have tried for many years and have failed to persuade him to not write so many or allow Mom and me to help him," Emma said shaking her head sadly.

"He didn't want your help?" James asked.

"No," Emma answered. "Growing up I guess I didn't seem to care because we were always so busy doing lots of other things. But after Dad's heart attack three years ago, my brother and I miss spending the time with my Dad. Even my Mom is concerned about how tired he gets spending all his time in his office writing. I just don't want him to regret that he didn't spend time with his family around the holidays, especially with my Mom."

Looking around the table, Emma realized the table went quiet. "I'm sorry, I didn't mean to be a downer."

"You're not," James said sincerely.

"I'm glad you told us," Mary said with a smile. "Why do you think your Dad started writing these letters?"

"That's a good question. He believes that he is doing God's will, but Mom and I are not convinced that is true anymore," Emma said.

"What do you mean?" James asked.

"When I was living in Florida teaching, the only way I got to see my parents was when they came to see me," Emma told them. "I was overwhelmed with what I was doing as a new teacher living in a new state. I remember once when my parents visited, my Dad told me that life is precious and that no one is guaranteed tomorrow. I had told him I was doing what God had called me to do. He agreed and told me that just because I was doing what God called me to do, it didn't mean that I should forget to spend time with the ones who love me."

"That is very good advice," Mary said.

The conversation ended as Mary got up to bring in the coffee and dessert. When dinner was over, Emma was helping Mary with the dishes when Emma's phone went off.

"Hi, Mom," Emma said. "Yes, I am still at Sam's. They invited me for dinner. No, you are not bothering me. What's up?"

"Could you please bring Dad's address book to school with you in the morning?" Ruth asked her. "Your Dad wants it back to make his phone calls."

"Sure, I will bring it to school tomorrow," Emma said. "Bye, Mom, I love you."

"Everything okay?" Mary asked.

"Yes, my Dad wants his address book back," Emma explained. "When I offered to write the letters for my Dad, Mom lent me his address book. Sam and I were going to input it all into the computer, so he could print off labels or change an address if he wanted."

"That's a great idea," Mary said.

"Well, Sam and I thought so, but my Dad wants no part of that," Emma said shaking her head. "I got the idea because Mom uses labels for all the cards or notes she sends out throughout the year."

"I knew I liked your mom, she is a smart woman," Mary smiled. "I do the same thing. I do not have the time to write out all of the Christmas cards by hand I send out every year."

"I wish my Dad felt that way, but he doesn't," Emma told her sadly.

The ladies finished up the dishes and made their way into the living room where Sam and his Dad were talking.

"It's getting late and we have school tomorrow, so I am going to head home," Emma told them. "Mary, James, it was nice meeting you. Thanks for dinner. Sam, I will see you at school in the morning."

"Emma, it was nice meeting you, too," James said warmly.

"Yes, thanks for coming," Mary added.

"Good night, Sam," Emma said as she zipped up her jacket and headed out the door to her car.

As she drove home, she heard the same song she had heard earlier on the radio, but this time she turned the music up so she could hear the words. Smiling, she realized the name of the song was, "Somebody's Angel."

Chapter 12

Once she got home, Emma made herself a cup of hot chocolate, sat down in her window seat, and stared out into the night. *I hope Dad knows what he is doing,* she told herself. Getting up and grabbing her journal, Emma wrote a page, closed the book, and smiled.

The next morning Emma rose early, grabbed her Dad's address book and left for school. Once she parked, she noticed Mom and Sam were already there.

Emma made her way down to see her Mom first.

"Morning, Mom," Emma said cheerfully.

"Good morning, Emma," her Mom said as she got up and hugged her daughter.

"Here's Dad's address book," Emma said handing it to her Mom.

"Thanks, but...," Ruth took it hesitantly.

"Mom, are you alright?" Emma asked, worried something else had happened.

"I'm fine," Ruth said. "I was just thinking."

"Thinking what?" Emma asked.

Quickly changing the subject, Ruth asked, "Did you get to meet Sam's parents last night?"

"Yes, I did," Emma smiled. "They're wonderful, just like you and Dad. Did you know that Sam's Mom could be an interior decorator?"

"No, I didn't," Ruth said.

"She really knows how to set a dining room table," Emma told her.

Emma took out her phone and showed her Mom the picture she took of Sam's dining room table.

"Wow!" Ruth exclaimed.

"That is exactly what I said," Emma said, knowing her Mom loved things like that.

"Do you think she would help me set our table for Thanksgiving?" Ruth asked Emma. "You did invite them, didn't you?"

"Oh, no, sorry, Mom, I forgot," Emma frowned. "Why don't you stop by after school today and ask them yourself and you can speak to Mary about the table."

"I'll do that," Ruth said with a smile.

The bell rang, so Emma gave her Mom a quick hug and said, "I need to go. Are we having lunch together?"

"Of course, why wouldn't we?" Ruth questioned.

"I just thought you would go home for lunch and see Dad," Emma said.

"No, not today!" Ruth said emphatically.

Emma noticed that her Mom's tone meant that there was something else going on and she didn't want to go home and check on her Dad.

"I'll see you at lunch, then," Emma said as she headed out the door.

Ruth smiled, sat down on her stool, and slid up to her computer.

I wonder why Mom doesn't want to go home? she thought to herself. *Hopefully I will find out more at lunch!*

The morning went by quickly and Josh never asked to go see her Mom, so it was turning out to be a good day. At lunch, Emma made her way down to the cafeteria and purchased a bowl of tomato soup and a grilled cheese sandwich. Spotting her Mom, Emma made her way over to their table where Ruth was talking to Jennifer.

"Hi, Jenn," Emma said. "Care to join us?"

"I would love to, but I have a lunch meeting," Jennifer said. "I will see you both later. Ruth, text me what you want me to bring Thanksgiving."

"Will do, Jenn," Ruth answered.

Jenn waved to her friend and walked away.

"Mom, you seem distracted," Emma said as she sampled her sandwich. "Is everything okay?"

"No, not really, but it will be," Ruth said with a sigh.

"Is there anything I can do?" Emma asked.

"Not yet, but I will let you know," Ruth promised.

"You're not eating?" Emma asked as she noticed her Mom only had a cup of hot tea.

"No, too much on my mind, but I am starting to feel better," Ruth told her.

"Hot tea," Emma said with a knowing smile.

"Hot tea," Ruth said grasping her mug.

As far back as Emma could remember, every time her Mom had a lot on her mind, she would fix herself a cup of Christmas tea with a slice of lemon. Her Mom loved her Christmas tea, even if it wasn't Christmas. Emma had to admit she herself kept a stash of Christmas tea at her condo as well.

"Mom, I told Dad I had four letters done. I already mailed the first two letters and have two more ready to go out in the mail," Emma explained. "Should I mail them or just throw them away?"

"Mail them!" Ruth said firmly.

"Are you sure?" Emma asked.

"I am," smiled Ruth.

"Alright, I will mail them after school," Emma said.

"Actually, would you mind getting me some stamps, too?" Ruth asked.

"Sure, how many do you want?" Emma asked her Mom.

"Five sheets should be enough," Ruth said after doing a quick calculation in her head.

"WOW! That's a lot of stamps," Emma commented.

"Yes, and I will use most of them," Ruth said with a smile.

"Do you want me to drop them off today?" Emma asked.

"You don't have to, I will leave that up to you," Ruth said. "I really won't need them for a day or so."

Just then Ruth's phone indicated she had gotten a text.

"It's Dad," Ruth told Emma. "I'll call him later."

"Is he okay?" Emma asked, wondering at her Mom's strange behavior.

"He wants his address book," Ruth answered grabbing her mug.

"I gave it to you this morning," Emma said, still disappointed she couldn't at least finish entering the information into the computer.

"You sound disappointed," Ruth said, taking a drink of her hot tea.

"I am, but it's what Dad wants," Emma said, blowing on her soup before she took a sip.

"I have an idea," Ruth said holding her mug with both hands. "After lunch, follow me down to my office."

"Okay," Emma said as she finished up her lunch.

Once they got to her office, Ruth took her husband's address book out of her school bag, took pictures of certain pages, and then handed the book back to Emma.

"What are you doing?" Emma asked.

"I'm giving you Dad's address book back because I want you to continue to add the names into your computer," Ruth told Emma.

"But Dad said he didn't want it," Emma protested.

"I know but he's wrong," Ruth said firmly.

"Mom, I don't want to make Dad any angrier," Emma said, biting her lip.

"You won't," Ruth told her confidently. "I will take care of your Dad."

"Isn't he going to need it to make his phone calls?" Emma asked, more confused than ever.

"No, I took pictures of the names he needs to call, so your Dad can do what he wants and you can still do what I want," Ruth smiled.

"And you want me to put his entire address book into the computer?" Emma asked, shaking her head.

"Yes, I do," Ruth said with a smile.

"It could take me a while," Emma said, looking at her watch.

"Take as long as you want," Ruth said as she hugged her daughter to reassure her that it would be alright. "There is really no rush. I know you have a very busy schedule coming up."

Walking away with the book, Emma wasn't sure what just happened, but she knew Mom was adamant about putting Dad's address book into her computer.

When school ended, Emma made her way down to Sam's office and peaked inside, "Hey, guess what?"

She showed him the address book.

"What happened?" Sam asked as he came out from behind his desk.

"Mom says to put it all on the computer," Emma said with a smile.

"What about your Dad?" Sam asked.

"Mom said she'll take care of it," Emma told him. "So, I'm leaving now. I need to go to the post office then home where I have some homework to do waving the book in her hand. Have a good night and say hello to your parents for me.

"I will," Sam told her, as confused as she was about what was going on.

When she got to the post office, she happened to run into Stacey Turner, Josh's mom.

"Emma, wait up," Stacey called out as she walked very slowly up to the door.

Emma opened the door for her and said, "Stacey, you look great."

"You are kind," Stacey said, trying to catch her breath. "Let's be honest, though, I'm as big as a house!"

"Yes, but a beautiful house," Emma said as they both laughed.

Emma hugged Stacey and asked again, "How are you feeling?"

"I am feeling like I want this kid out of me," Stacey said. "I want to see my feet again and wear pretty shoes."

Emma knew Stacey loved shoes. Before she got pregnant, she would wear beautiful shoes with high heels. Emma always wondered how she could walk so quickly in them. The joke between them was that if Emma ever tried to walk in Stacey's shoes, she would fall right over and her class would have to catch her.

"You will be back in pretty shoes soon enough," Emma said walking next to her.

"Josh told me you are writing Christmas Letters this year instead of sending out Christmas cards," Stacey said.

"Well, I was going to, but not anymore," Emma said sadly, shaking her head as they waited in line at the Post Office counter.

"If you don't mind me asking, are these the same Christmas Letters your Dad writes?" Stacey asked her.

"Yes," Emma told her friend. "I tried to write like my Dad since he broke his arm, but I couldn't, so I'm not writing anymore."

"Why not?" Stacey asked, leaning against the counter trying to get comfortable.

"Long story, but not to worry, my Dad is taking his project back," Emma said. "Since he can't write them out, he's going to call those who are on his list this year."

"Oh, I see," Stacey said rather sadly.

"Is there something wrong, Stacey?" Emma asked, suddenly wondering how she knew about the letters in the first place.

"No, I'm just surprised that's all," Stacey admitted.

"I was only doing it because I thought that is what he would have wanted," Emma said. "But I was wrong. They are his letters."

"Well, I have to tell you, my husband and I received one of your Dad's Letters last year and it made our Christmas," Stacey told her. "In fact, I still have it. It was the most beautiful letter I have ever received. I will cherish it until the day I die!"

"Really?" Emma said, surprised. "I had no idea you received one of Dad's Letters."

"When we are done here, follow me to my car," Stacey said to Emma.

"Okay," Emma said as they each finished their Post Office business.

Stacey finished up first, so when Emma went outside she did not see Stacey. Then she heard a car horn. Stacey had pulled her car up directly in front of her.

"Emma, come sit inside for a minute," Stacey invited.

Emma jumped in Stacey's car, "Are you alright? Are you in labor?"

"I'm fine, but what I am about to share with you is private," Stacey told her. "Last year, two days before Christmas, my mom died."

"I am so sorry, I had no idea," Emma said compassionately.

"No one did," Stacey explained. "We kept it quiet. For Josh's sake, Santa came and we celebrated, but I can tell you, I did not want to celebrate Christmas. If it had been up to me, the holiday would have come and gone without me batting an eye. But your Dad reminded me and my husband that Christmas was not about us, it was about giving. So, we gave Josh the Christmas a little boy deserves."

"How did Dad remind you?" Emma asked. "Was it in one of his Letters?"

"I'll never forget it," Stacey said with tears in her eyes. "We were running late and by the time we got to church that night, the church was packed. Somehow your Dad happen to turn around and summoned us to sit in the pew right in front of them. I was good until the kids walked up the aisle and placed baby Jesus in the manger."

"I just lost it in church," Stacey shared. "My husband tried to console me, but he didn't know what to do. Josh was starting to get upset watching me, so I just excused myself and ran to the bathroom. Well, your mom followed me. I don't know why, but I told her everything and she listened."

"Mom is a good listener," Emma said with a smile.

"Yes, just like my mom was," Stacey shared.

Emma could not help the tears that were welling up in her own eyes.

"After I told her everything, somehow, I felt better," Stacey said with a smile. "She must have told your Dad because the next day, they both came over and your Dad gave me a letter. I still have it locked away. I will cherish it forever. When Josh and this little one are older, I will share it with them, too."

"I don't know what to say," Emma said, wiping a tear from her cheek.

"Emma, I'm sorry you're not writing the Christmas Letters for your Dad, but I guess a call is better than nothing," Stacey said sadly, rubbing her belly.

"You don't sound convinced Stacey," Emma said.

"I'm really not," Stacey admitted. "Receiving a Christmas Letter is special."

"I only wrote four," Emma told her. "As I wrote them, I realized I needed to send my own message and not think about what Dad would write."

"How did you know what to write, if I can ask?" Stacey asked.

"I gave each name to God and He gave me the words to write," Emma shared, realizing she was truly disappointed not to be writing any more letters.

"I'm sure you did great," Stacey told her.

"I hope so. Even with all the thought and prayer I put into each one, I know that I am not a writer," Emma admitted.

"Well, you don't have to be," Stacey said firmly. "God gives us all kinds of gifts and yours is definitely serving others."

"Oh, I don't think of teaching as serving others," Emma said with a smile. "I just love it!"

"Sure, it is! You do a lot more than you know," Stacey assured her. "In fact, I would say you are an angel."

"An angel?" Emma said with a little laugh.

"Yes, I have seen you convince a particular five-year-old that staying in class is important," Stacey told her.

Knowing Stacey was talking about Josh, Emma admitted, "Well, I guess I have with my students, but the way I handled the Dad's letters was wrong, so I gave Dad a choice."

"Really?" Stacey asked.

"Yes, I told him I could write the remaining Letters or he could make calls. He chose to make phone calls," Emma explained.

Hesitating, Stacey asked, "Did you know that the Letters your Dad has written have changed people's lives?"

Not knowing what to say, Emma nodded and said, "I'm sure they did. He always puts a lot of time into them!"

"Anyway, I am grateful for your parents and I just wanted you to know how blessed you are to have them," Stacey told her. "Cherish them for no one knows what tomorrow brings."

"Thank you for sharing with me, Stacey," Emma said.

"You're welcome," Stacey said with a big smile. "By the way, how is Josh doing? Is he staying in your class?"

Smiling as she got out of Stacey's car, Emma nodded, "Yes, he is."

"That's great!" Stacey said as she backed up and drove off.

Emma stood there and watched her car pull away thinking about what Stacey had said, *Angel, I think not!* Emma shook her head as she made her way to her car. She turned up the radio and heard a familiar Christmas song. *Wasn't that the same one she had heard earlier?* she thought.

After she fixed herself some dinner, she made her way over to her computer with her Dad's address book. Seeing the post-it note on a page, Emma smiled, grateful that Sam marked where she needed to resume her task.

Emma sat and worked for a couple of hours, and marked her page before she headed to bed.

Remembering her conversation with Stacey, she decided to text Mom, "Do you remember Stacey Wilson, Josh's mom from my class?"

"Yes, how is she doing?" her Mom responded.

Emma typed, "She's good, she's anxious for her son to get here. She says she misses seeing her feet and buying pretty shoes. I ran into her at the Post Office and she told me what happened last year. You will be happy to know that she still has the letter Dad wrote to her and her husband."

Adding a smiley face, she added, "She thinks you're both great."

Ruth smiled when she read that and sent a smiley face back, "She's a smart woman."

"Yes, she is!" Emma typed. "She also told me that Dad's Letter changed their lives. Mom, do you think the people who are getting a phone call this year from Dad will feel like their lives have changed?"

"No," is all Ruth could type.

"Mom, I'm not sure Dad making phone calls is the right thing to do," Emma wrote.

"Neither do I," Mom wrote back.

Emma typed, "Good night. I love you," and put her phone on the table. She made herself a cup of hot chocolate and got out her journal. Then she wrote as she sat in her window seat.

When she was finished, she picked up her phone and called Jennifer. She had a lot on her mind and knew she would not be able to pull this off without the help from her best friend.

"Hi, Jenn," Emma said. "I have something to run by you. You got a few minutes to talk?"

As Emma and Jennifer talked, it became clear what they needed to do.

"You're crazy, but it's a good idea," Jennifer said to her.

"I know, but just think, Jenn, what a great way to start off the holiday season," Emma said excitedly.

"I'll get right on it," Jennifer told her friend. "Come by my office first thing tomorrow, okay?"

"I will and thanks, Jenn," Emma said gratefully. "I owe you one."

"Yes, you do!" Jennifer laughed.

Looking up to heaven, Emma spoke quietly, "Lord, thank You for Jennifer. I am blessed to call her my friend. She's the best. Amen."

Getting up from her window seat, Emma made her way into her bedroom where she fell on her bed, with a heavy sigh.

Emma looked up again, "Three days until Thanksgiving, Lord, can I really pull this off?"

Chapter 13

The day before Thanksgiving was only a half day of school, so the morning went by very quickly. As Emma sat at her desk, she thought about the last two days and what a blur they had been.

"Knock! Knock!"

Emma looked up, "Stacey, it's good to see you, thank you for coming in."

"My husband said you needed to speak to me and it was important," Stacey said. "What has Josh done?"

"Nothing, I promise he has not been down to see Mom all week," Emma said with a smile.

Looking around to find a seat she could fit in, Stacey asked, "Is this going to take long because if it is, I need a real chair."

"Funny you say that," Emma laughed. "I have just the right chair for you. I'll be right back."

Emma walked into the classroom connected to hers and wheeled out a huge office chair on wheels decorated with blue balloons. Every mom whose child was in her class along with some of the teachers started yelling, "Surprise!"

Stacey could not believe her eyes. As Emma wheeled Stacey down to the gym, a smile came across her face. She and the other teachers had pulled off a surprise baby shower in three days. There was a huge cake, balloons, goody bags, and gifts for Stacey and a couple of other moms who were also pregnant in Emma's class as well.

As the party was wrapping up, Sam and Stacey's husband made an appearance.

"I don't know how you did it, Emma, but thank you," Stacey's husband said, giving her a big hug. "This has been quite a roller coaster ride for us. This is exactly what Stacey needed."

"You, too, I hope," Emma said, laughing happily. "You have a lot of gifts to go through. From all of the clothes I have seen, your son is going to have quite a wardrobe for a while."

"That is fine with me!" the proud papa said.

"Why don't I help you get all of this out to your car," Sam offered.

"I'm not sure this is all going to fit," Stacey's husband said.

"It's okay," Sam told him. "I have a truck and whatever doesn't fit, I'll throw in my truck and follow you home."

Sam smiled at Emma as if to say, "Great job!"

Emma smiled as she turned to face Stacey.

"I do not have the words right now, but I know the Lord will give them to me when it's time. All I can say is thank you!" Stacey said as she hugged Emma tightly. "You are an angel and Josh is so blessed to have you as his teacher. I pray you will be here to teach our new son as well."

"I am not going anywhere. It would be my pleasure to teach Josh's little brother!" Emma told Stacey.

"Well, that was quite a day," Ruth said, helping Emma clean up after the baby shower.

"Yes, it was," Emma said with a tired smile. "Thanks for all of your help, Mom. I don't know what I would have done without you!"

Pulling her mom into a hug, Emma said, "Mom, I want you to know, I never take you for granted. I am so thankful you are my mom and I love you very much."

Ruth was speechless for a few seconds, "Thanks, Emma, you have no idea how much I needed to hear that. Stacey is right, you are an angel!"

"No, Mom, you're an angel," Emma said giving her mom another big hug.

"Emma," yelled Sam. "We have everything loaded up. Can you tell Jennifer that I am going to follow them home? The high chair and stroller didn't fit in their trunk."

Waving, Emma yelled back, "I'll tell her and thanks Sam for all of your help."

"Not a problem, see you all later and Happy Thanksgiving," Sam yelled as he pulled out of the parking lot.

The other teachers yelled, "Happy Thanksgiving."

"Well ladies, our holiday season has officially begun," Jennifer said with a smile. "I hope you all have a wonderful Thanksgiving and I will see you all next Monday."

Emma watched as Jennifer hugged her mom, "Ruth, what time would you like us to come over on Thanksgiving?"

"How about eleven o clock?" Ruth suggested. "You can help Mary set the table."

"We'll be there!" Jennifer said as she headed out to her car.

When Ruth got home she was in a great mood. She was determined she was not going to let Frank ruin it for her.

"Ruth, did you get my address book?" he yelled from the living room.

Ruth did not answer.

"Ruth!" Frank yelled again.

Then he got up and came out into the kitchen, "Didn't you hear me?"

"I did," Ruth answered calmly.

"Then why didn't you answer?" he asked her angrily.

Looking at her husband, she asked, "Are you sure you didn't hit your head when you fell?"

"I'm sure, why?" Frank asked.

"Then you must be getting senile," Ruth declared.

"What are you talking about, Ruth?" he asked her, clearly irritated.

"Frank Trask, did you forget that I do not answer when you yell to me from another room?" Ruth reminded him.

"You're right," Frank admitted. "Did you get my address book?"

"No!" Ruth told him.

"Did Emma forgot to bring it to school?" Frank asked. "I texted her and told her not to forget."

"She didn't forget," Ruth said calmly.

"Ruth, where is my book?" Frank demanded.

"Emma, has it," Ruth answered.

"She didn't give it to you?" Frank asked.

"Yes, she did, but I gave it back to her," Ruth told him.

Frank's face turned red as he yelled, "You did what?"

"I gave it back to her," Ruth repeated.

"How am I going to make calls if I don't have phone numbers?" Frank asked angrily.

"Oh? You want phone numbers," Ruth asked.

"Of course, I do!" Frank said, getting more and more irritated.

"Then why didn't you say so?" Ruth asked him.

Picking up her phone, she started pushing buttons.

"What are you doing now?" he asked her.

"I'm sending you the phone numbers of the people you are going to call," Ruth explained patiently.

"What?" Frank asked, his mouth open in disbelief.

"What part of that did you not understand?" Ruth asked.

"I need my address book," he said, raising his voice.

"No, you don't," Ruth said calmly. "You need phone numbers and that is what I am giving you."

"By the way, I don't appreciate your tone," Ruth told him after sending him the list. "And another thing, if you want to see your address book ever again, you will speak to me the way you have always done before, with respect. Do you understand me?"

Frank had very seldom seen her like this and knew she meant business, "I'll be in my office, please let me know when dinner is ready."

Frank sat down at his desk and wondered why he was acting the way he was. Then he thought, *I do know why*. He slammed his left hand onto his desk and looked down at his cast. God had taken his writing away and this made Frank question why. He knew there would be no peace until he found the answer to that question.

The next morning when Frank woke up, he realized that Ruth was not in bed next to him.

"Ruth?" he called, but there was no answer.

Grabbing his robe, he called again as he made his way into the kitchen.

"I'm in here," she called from the living room.

"What are you doing sitting in the dark?" Frank asked.

"I must have fallen asleep out here," Ruth said as she stretched and started to get up. "Do you want some coffee?"

"You stay put, I'll make it," Frank said, as he turned around and walked into the kitchen.

"What did you say?" Ruth asked.

"I said, stay put, I'll bring you a cup," Frank called to her.

"Are you sure you can?" Ruth asked as she started to get up again.

"I've got this," he called. "Ruth Ann, I can see you, sit down."

When Frank brought his wife her coffee, she did not know what to think or say, "Thank you, Frank!"

"You're welcome, but you really need to start drinking your coffee black," Frank said with a smile.

"Why?" she asked curiously.

"Because it's easier to fix," he said and they both laughed.

"Frank, are you saying I'm high maintenance?" Ruth asked teasingly.

"When it comes to your coffee you are," he smiled. "I had to get the caramel creamer out of the refrigerator and add a touch of sugar, too. With mine I just had to put the cup of dark roast in the machine and push a button."

"You seem to be able to handle it alright," Ruth said, taking a sip of her coffee. "I'm proud of you, Frank, thank you."

"I didn't know if I could do anything or maybe I was just babying myself because I felt sorry for myself," he admitted.

"What's going on?" Ruth asked him, wrapping her hands around her coffee mug. "Last night you were very angry when you went to bed."

Putting his cup down, Frank made his way over to the other rocking chair and sat next to his wife.

"When I realized that you weren't coming to bed, I couldn't sleep, so I got up and God and I had a long talk," Frank told her. "I don't know how long I sat there because I must have fallen asleep as I woke up in the chair."

"Ruth, I am so sorry for the way I have been acting," he said, turning to look at her. "I was mad at God for taking my Christmas Letters."

"They're not **your** letters," Ruth said as she reached out and grabbed her husband's hand. "They're God's."

"I know," Frank admitted. "He told me that last night. I am ashamed of the way I have been treating you, Ben, and Emma. None of you deserve that."

"No, we don't, but I understand why you felt the way you did," Ruth told him. "I'm sorry I did not show you the compassion you needed. I wasn't being very understanding and for that, I'm sorry."

"It sounds like God spoke to both of us last night," Frank said with a smile.

"He sure did!" Ruth smiled as well. "Isn't it amazing that He can talk to both of us at the same time and He knows exactly what to say?"

"We have an amazing God!" Frank said.

"Yes, we do," Ruth agreed.

They sat silently until the phone rang and startled both of them.

Ruth reached over to answer the phone, "Hello, Happy Thanksgiving to you, too, Mrs. Jones. Yes, he's here, just a moment."

"Frank, Mrs. Jones wants to talk to you," Ruth said.

Covering the phone, Frank whispered, "She's on the list."

"Good morning, Mrs. Jones, Happy Thanksgiving!" Frank said.

Ruth made herself busy in the kitchen, thinking, *Mrs. Jones must have received Emma's letter yesterday.* Ruth looked up to heaven and prayed, *God, I hope you gave Emma the words Mrs. Jones needed to hear.*

Emma woke up and wasted no time looking outside. It was bright and sunny. *I guess we're not getting snow, but at least the temperature is cold,* she thought. Feeling a little disappointed, Emma made her way to her kitchen and made herself her breakfast and a cup of coffee. Sitting back down in her window seat, she got out her Bible and her journal. Emma sat and stared outside. Not realizing a couple of hours had passed, she jumped up and got ready to make her way over to her parents' house for fun, food, football, and watching the Macy's Thanksgiving Day parade. *It's going to be a great day,* she said to herself as she made her way to her car.

It was supposed to snow, though, she said as she looked up, but she smiled when she felt the warm sun on her face.

Turning on her radio, the song which she had heard so many times this holiday season came on again. *It seems like every time I get in the car, they play it. They really need to play a different song once in a while,* she thought as she changed stations. However, since it was now officially the Christmas season, she could not get used to the other music. Shaking her head, she turned the radio back on the Christmas station as she drove to her parents' home.

Ben came outside to greet her, "What's wrong with Dad?"

"I don't know, why?" Emma asked him.

"Because he just bit my head off after I said that Dallas wasn't going to win this year," Ben told her, shaking his head.

"Well, you know how Dad feels about the Cowboys," Emma pointed out as she got out of the car and gave her brother a hug.

"Yes, but that's not it," Ben said. "We can usually joke about football, but not today. He's in one foul mood. Are you still writing his Christmas Letters?"

"No, in fact, he was happy when I told him I would give them up and he can make phone calls instead," Emma explained.

"Well, I don't know what it is, but watch yourself," Ben warned.

"Let's go see if Mom knows something," Emma suggested.

Her Mom was in the kitchen and had already put the turkey into the oven.

"It smells good in here," Emma said with a smile.

"Emma, great you're here!" Ruth said giving her daughter a hug.

"Where's Dad?" Emma asked.

"He's in his office," Ruth answered.

"I'll go say hello and then come back and give you a hand," Emma said, as she headed for her dad's office.

Knocking on the door to his office, Emma peaked in and said, "Happy Thanksgiving, Dad!"

"Happy Thanksgiving, Emma," he said.

Emma could tell something was bothering her Dad, so she asked, "Are you okay?"

"I'm fine," he responded.

"Are you sure?" Emma said worriedly. "You seem out of sorts."

"I'm just tired. I didn't sleep very well," he told her.

"Can I get you anything?" Emma offered.

"Yes, you could give me my address book," he said.

Surprised, Emma didn't know what to say.

"Mom told me to keep it," Emma finally told him.

"I know, never mind," he said irritably.

"I'm going to go help Mom, then," Emma said shaking her head sadly.

"Yeah, you go do that," was his grumpy response.

Emma made her way back into the kitchen, "Mom, Dad just asked me for his address book."

"Figures, what did you tell him?" her mom asked.

"I told him you told me to keep it," Emma answered.

"Good girl!" Ruth said.

"Mom, I don't want to get in the middle of whatever this is," Emma said carefully.

"Emma, trust me, I have a plan," Ruth told her confidently. "Now, I need your help. Please start by peeling those potatoes."

For the rest of the morning and into afternoon, Emma and her Mom cooked and tasted all the great foods they had prepared. Jennifer and her family and then Sam and his parents came over midafternoon. Mary helped by setting the dining room table.

"Mary, the table looks beautiful!" Ruth exclaimed happily. "You have the gift!"

"Oh, it's nothing," Mary said, though obviously pleased with Ruth's approval. "What else can I help you with?"

Admiring the dining room table, gave Emma an idea and said, "Mary, when you're done, can I see you a moment?"

"Sure, let me finish these dishes and then I will come find you," Mary said.

I wonder what that is all about? Ruth thought as she watched Emma pull Mary outside to the swing.

"Frank," James said, "it is nice to meet you."

"You, too," Frank said, shaking hands. "I'm sorry I didn't greet you the other day."

"It's okay," James said kindly. "I am sorry about your arm."

"Me, too," Frank said shaking his head. "I never really appreciated the use of both of my arms until I couldn't use this one."

"I know what you mean," James told him. "A couple of years ago when we were living in Colorado, I forgot to sand our front steps. I fell and broke my leg. I was in a cast up to my thigh. It was awful!"

"It sounds awful!" Frank told him sincerely. "Did you have trouble sleeping?"

"Big time!" James admitted. "I slept in a recliner for six weeks. I promised myself I would pay more attention to the weather after that."

"When do you get your permanent cast on?" James asked Frank noticing he was still in a temporary cast.

"Tomorrow," Frank told him.

"That will make your life easier," James assured him.

"I hope so," Frank said.

"Dinner is ready, so let's eat," Ruth called and they all quickly came to the table.

"Frank, will you bless this food?" Ruth asked.

"I think James should do it since he is our guest," Frank said.

Feeling a little embarrassed at Frank's refusal to pray, Ruth asked, "James, would you mind?"

"Not at all, let us all join hands and pray," James graciously answered.

As they ate, the atmosphere was light, and everybody seemed to enjoy themselves, even Frank.

However, as the day went on, Emma sensed that something was still bothering her Dad. The four letters that she had written were out and he had all the phone numbers he needed for his calls. *You would think having his project back he would be happy*, she thought.

Sam approached her and quietly asked, "Are you okay?"

"Something is wrong with Dad," Emma answered in a whisper.

"I know what you mean," Sam admitted. "He seems to be distracted about something."

"I know, I'm glad I'm not the only one who has noticed," Emma told him.

"It's obvious that something is bothering him," Sam agreed.

"I'm going to go talk to him," Emma said.

"Maybe it's not the best time," Sam suggested. "Let him enjoy the rest of the game and when my parents and I leave then ask him."

"Well, maybe you're right," Emma said.

"Look at him," Sam pointed out. "He and my father are enjoying the game and each other's company."

Emma smiled and said, "Look at our moms, they haven't stopped talking since your mother got here!"

"I know," Sam laughed.

Turning around and looking up into his face, she said warmly, "I'm glad you and your family are here. This has been the best Thanksgiving I have had in a while."

"Me, too," Sam said, smiling back at her.

When the game was over, everyone said their goodbyes, Jennifer and family left, and Sam and his parents went back to his house.

Emma wasted no time in seeking out her Dad and asking him what was wrong.

"Emma, come sit down," her dad said in a very serious voice.

Emma sat down across from her Dad. Something in his voice scared Emma.

"Do you remember when you told me that you were going to write the Letters?" he asked her.

"How can I forget? You were so angry with me," Emma said with a shiver.

"Yes, I was," he said reluctantly. "but I should not have taken my anger out on you for you are not the one who made me angry."

Looking her straight in her eyes, he admitted sadly, "Emma, I was mad at God."

"Why?" Emma asked, totally taken back by what her dad had just said.

"Because He took my writing away from me," Frank answered, then added, "and what happened many years ago."

"Dad," Emma said shaking her head. "I don't believe God took your writing away from you."

"Oh yes, He did," Frank said firmly. "You even said so yourself that maybe my fall was a sign that God did not want me to write Christmas Letters anymore."

Not knowing how to respond, Emma sat quietly and waited for her dad to continue.

"Emma, that is what He did," Frank finally said. "In fact, I think I knew last year when it took me so long to get my Letters out and your Mom had to threaten to burn all of my paper and even my address book that maybe I was holding on to it a little too long. But I didn't want to believe it. I knew the Letters would help those who needed it, but maybe I was doing it for all of the wrong reasons."

"What reasons?" Emma asked sensing her Dad had something really important to tell her.

"That is not important," Frank said waving his hand. "But I am beginning to see that God does have a plan. It's a different one than I wanted, and at first, I did not want to accept that. Then after talking to your Mom last night, I am seeing a lot clearer now."

"I don't understand," Emma said, moving to sit on the floor at her dad's feet.

"You came over the other day, and with dignity I might add, gave me an option," Frank said with a smile. "You offered to continue to write the remaining Letters or I could call the people instead."

"Yes, and you told me and Mom that you wanted to make calls," Emma said.

"That's right, but Emma I was wrong," Dad told her. "Let me explain, we received two calls regarding the letters you mailed. The first call came from Mrs. Jones saying that we must be so proud of our daughter. Your letter touched her heart. I told her that you had no idea what the circumstances were, but you prayed and God gave you the words. Mrs. Jones could not understand how you knew exactly what to say, but told me your letter said everything she needed to hear. It gave her hope for what she is going through."

Emma just shook her head in amazement as tears formed in her eyes.

"The second call came from Mr. Sendler," Frank said. "He accused me of telling you his situation. I told him like I did Mrs. Jones, that you did not know his situation and that you prayed and God gave you the words. Mr. Sendler became very quiet on the phone and said that your letter confirmed what God had asked him to do."

"What did God ask him to do?" Emma asked.

"I don't know, he didn't say," Frank answered. "He did say he was reluctant, but now he is sure he's ready to do God's will."

"I can't believe it!" Emma said shaking her head in awe.

"I can," Ruth said, sitting by her husband.

"Emma, you were supposed to write these Letters this year and I have taken it away from you and I shouldn't have. I'm so sorry!" Frank said with tears in his eyes. "I am so proud of you. Will you please write the remaining six letters and write what God puts into your heart?"

Tears filled her eyes as Emma answered, "Of course, Dad, I will be happy to. I admit, though, I was relieved that you wanted to make the calls because writing is really not my scene. I only did it so you wouldn't mope around the house during the holidays."

"Emma, I have faith in you and apparently so does God," Dad said smiling at her.

"But I don't really like writing," Emma told them.

"Well, sometimes God calls us to do things we don't want to do to make us strong," he told her.

"Maybe next year you and Mom can work on them together?" Emma suggested.

"I'm not planning that far in advance," he said with a smile. "God might have another project for me and your Mom."

"Okay, Dad, I will write the rest of the Letters," Emma smiled. "I am so glad there are only six left though."

"Great!" Frank said. "Now that we have that out of the way, we can really start the holiday season."

"Not quite," Emma said. "I'm still concerned about something else you said, Dad. You said you were mad at God for what He did years ago. What did you mean?"

"Nothing has ever gotten passed you, has it, Emma", her dad said with a smile.

Turning to his wife, Frank asked, "What do you think, Ruth, is she ready?"

"Absolutely!" Ruth answered. "I'll be right back."

Ruth left the living room, went into the office, and returned with a faded envelope.

Sitting again next to her husband, Ruth took a breath, and said, "The year before you were born, I had a miscarriage. Your Dad and I were starting to think we would never have children. The miscarriage happened three days before Christmas, so your Dad and I decided that we couldn't celebrate Christmas that year."

Emma could not believe what she was hearing. Her parents loved Christmas and they had always celebrated the holiday with anticipation. She could not imagine her parents cancelling Christmas.

"We were so excited about that Christmas. We were going to have a son. If he had lived, he would have been our Christmas miracle, but God had other plans. Your Dad and I were so devastated, and our families were so heartbroken, we just could not celebrate.

So, your Dad called everyone and told them that we were not celebrating Christmas and all festivities were cancelled."

Getting on her knees in front of her Mom, tears fell down Emma's face.

"Mom, I am so sorry," Emma said sadly.

"I still think about him every Christmas and then I am reminded of what happened next," Ruth told Emma.

"Christmas Eve came and we turned off all of the Christmas lights outside. We did not go to church and we took down our Christmas tree," Ruth admitted sadly.

"You didn't go to church?" Emma said, shaking her head in unbelief. "As far back as I can remember, you have never missed a Christmas Eve service."

"That was the only year that we have not attended a Christmas Eve service," Ruth admitted.

"It's hard for me to imagine you both skipping church," Emma told them.

"Emma, when you have gone through a personally devastating loss like your Dad and I did, your mind can make you do some foolish things," Ruth told her, shaking her head sadly.

"I had no idea," Emma said. "Why haven't you ever shared this with me before?"

"It never seemed like the right time until now. You have asked me numerous times over the years why I write the Letters. This is why," Frank said, leaning closer to his daughter and handing her a letter. "Around eight o'clock that Christmas Eve, the doorbell rang. We weren't expecting anybody, so we had no idea who it could be. When I opened the door, there stood Mr. Pretzel, our next-door neighbor."

"I don't remember him," Emma said.

"I'm sure you don't, he moved to Florida the following Summer," Frank said. "Anyway, there I was in my pajamas and there stood Mr. Pretzel, the meanest neighbor on our street. I swear, I never saw that man smile."

"Hello, Mr. Pretzel," I said. "He handed me this letter and said, 'Frank, this is for you and your wife.' Then he turned and walked back to his house."

"I'll never forget it," Frank said shaking his head. "It was raining and Mr. Pretzel was soaking wet because he did not have an umbrella. Strange as it sounds, he didn't seem to mind and walked back to his house slowly, looking up at the sky."

"Open the letter, but please be careful with it," Ruth told her.

Emma opened the envelope and began to read:

Dear Frank and Ruth,

I am sorry for your loss and I know you are hurting, but what gives you the right to cancel Christmas? I think you both need a reminder of what Christmas is really about. It is about a little baby boy born in a stable many years ago. Christmas is not about us or the presents we receive. It is about what we can give to others. God gave us His most precious gift, His Son. So, at Christmas, don't you think that we should give something back to Him? I wish you and your wife a Merry Christmas.

Mr. Pretzel

Emma carefully folded the letter, put it back into the envelope, and handed it to her Mom saying nothing. She looked up at her Dad who had tears in his eyes.

"As I watched him walk back to his house in the rain, I could not imagine what he had written to us," Frank told Emma. "But after your Mom and I read his letter, we were not only reminded what Christmas is all about, we felt ashamed. Deep down we knew God had a special place in Heaven for our son. We were being selfish, and from that Christmas on, no matter what was going on in our lives, we made sure that we gave back to others especially at Christmas."

"The Letters were my way of giving back," Frank explained. "When I fell and broke my arm, I felt like God just ripped it out of my hands and that hurt. When your Mom and I talked last night, she reminded me these letters aren't mine at all, they are God's. I'm was just His messenger, so now it is your turn, Emma."

"What about next year?" Emma asked.

"We'll have to wait and see, but I'm not worried," Frank said with a big smile. "This year, this time is what matters."

"I am so glad you shared this with me," Emma said sincerely. "I love you both so much!"

Emma rose to her knees and hugged and kissed both of her parents.

"I don't know about the two of you, but it has been quite a day," Frank said with a yawn. "I'm bushed and I need to rest this arm, so I am off to bed."

"I'm pretty tired, too," Ruth said. "Emma, why don't you stay, it's late?"

"Thanks, I will, but I'm not tired yet, so I'm going to sit here awhile," Emma said and rose to hug her mom again.

"Good night, Mom."

"Good night, Emma."

Chapter 14

As Emma sat in the dark staring at the fire, the Christmas song that she had heard so many times the last few days came on the radio Mom had left playing softly. As she quietly listened to the lyrics, she remembered what her Dad said about how we should all want to give something back to God for what He has given to us.

"Okay, God, how can I give back?" she whispered.

The Letters are really Dad's, Emma thought. *I want to do something else, but what?*

As the song ended, Emma drifted off to sleep with a smile on her face.

"Emma," her mom said as she shook her awake.

Opening her eyes, she answered, "Hi, Mom."

"Aren't you due at Sam's for lunch, today?" Mom asked her.

"Yes," Emma answered smiling.

"Well, you better get a move on, it's nearly ten now," Ruth warned her.

"Ten!" Emma yelled jumping up and almost falling over. "I need to get home and change!"

"Well then, you better get a move on," Mom said, laughing.

Emma smiled and hugged her Mom.

She quickly put on her shoes, grabbed her coat, and was about to head out of the door when she asked, "Where's Dad?"

"He's in the kitchen," Ruth told her.

Running into the kitchen, Emma asked, "Dad, where's your pen?"

"It's in the top right drawer of my desk," he answered.

"Is it still okay if I use it?" she asked.

"Yes, of course," Frank said with a smile.

Running into the office, Emma opened the drawer and took out the pen.

Opening the pen box, Emma smiled, "You and I have a lot of work to do."

She closed the box and went back to the kitchen.

Grabbing her Dad's face with both of her hands, she said, "Dad, thank you!"

She ran out the door and into her car. Turning up the radio, she heard the same song again she'd heard last night as she had drifted off to sleep.

Emma smiled and looked up to heaven and said, "You've got this?"

When she reached her condo, Emma grabbed the pen and went inside. She freshened up, placed the pen beside her Dad's address book, and headed to Sam's.

When Sam opened the door, she apologized, "I'm sorry I'm late, I overslept."

"You're not that late, come on in," Sam said with a smile.

Sam looked at Emma and could tell that there was something different.

"What is it?" he asked.

"We need to talk later," Emma said. "Don't worry, it's good, but I do need your help."

"Okay," Sam smiled. "Come on in, Mother and Father want to speak to you about a tree."

"Hi, Emma, we're going to go get a tree today," Mary explained. "Would you like to join us after lunch?"

"I would, but unfortunately, I have to pass," Emma explained. "I have Christmas business to attend to."

"That sounds intriguing," James said, as he ushered everyone into the dining room for lunch.

"It's my Dad," Emma said excitedly. "He has given me permission to write the rest of the Christmas Letters."

"WOW!" Sam said. "I thought he was going to make calls instead."

"He changed his mind," Emma said with a big smile.

"What about his address book?" Sam asked.

"That is where you come in," Emma said. "If you have the time, I would like the rest of them entered before Christmas. Mom suggested it would be a great gift for Dad, but I don't think I can do both."

"I can help with that," Sam agreed with a smile.

"Thanks, Sam," Emma said with a smile, thinking one more thing off my to do list.

During lunch, they spoke about Christmas and the traditions they all had.

"Mary, remember we started talking yesterday about your lovely table designs?" Emma said. "We never got to have our private discussion yesterday. Well, I have an idea I think you can help me with."

"Sure, what can I do?" Mary asked as she and Emma made their way into Sam's kitchen with the lunch dishes.

"Mom was so impressed with your dining room table yesterday, I was wondering if you would decorate Mom's table for Christmas, but the catch is I would like it to be a surprise."

"I would love to, but how are we going to pull that off?" Mary asked, intrigued with the idea.

"I don't know yet, but I am sure if we put our heads together, we can come up with something," Emma smiled. "Mary, I can't wait to see the look on her face when she sees it. I'll check my calendar and give you a call later this afternoon. Thank you for agreeing to help me with this!"

"It's my pleasure, Emma," Mary smiled. "It will be fun!"

"Mother," Sam called. "Father is ready to go when you are."

"Are you sure you can't join us?" Mary asked.

"I really need to get home, but you know, an hour out if the fresh air might be exactly what I need to get the rest of the Letters done," Emma reasoned. "I'm in, let's go!"

"Great," Sam said when they told him Emma was joining them.

Emma could not explain why, but she was having the time of her life

When they reached the farm, they bundled up and made their way to the hay wagon that would take them out to the field of trees.

"Do you know what type of tree you are looking for?" Emma asked.

"I don't since this is the first time I have done this," Sam told her.

"You are in for a treat," Emma told them. "My parents and I have been coming out here for years. They have either Virginia Pine or Leyland Cypress trees. Both are beautiful."

Jumping off the wagon, Sam grabbed a measuring stick and James grabbed a hand saw and they walked toward the trees.

"There are so many!" Mary said, looking around at all the beautiful trees.

"Yes, but when you really look closely, you will find out that some have crooked trunks and you don't want that, so take your time," Emma advised.

As they started looking around, Emma took in the sight and scent of the trees. The temperature was crisp and dry. With the sun shining, it was a beautiful day.

"What about this one?" James called.

They all went over to check it out.

"Emma," James asked. "What do you think?"

"Well, it is lovely on this side, but the hole on the other side might be a problem," she pointed out. "You would have to position it to make sure that side was where no one ever sees it."

"Good point," James agreed.

"Emma, why don't you and Sam make your way down that row and Mary and I will look this way," James suggested.

Sam and Emma looked at tree after tree.

"What made your Dad change his mind about the Christmas Letters?" Sam asked.

Not wanting to convey all that her parents had shared with her, Emma simply said, "Mom and Dad talked for a while the night before and it dawned on Dad that the Letters were not really his."

"Not his?" Sam asked.

"No, they belong to God" Emma tried to explain. "Dad came to realization that he was to be the messenger for God."

"Something tells me that there is more to it than that," Sam smiled. "But I won't pry."

"I appreciate that," Emma smiled.

"I just think it's great that you'll be writing them," Sam said. "And that he gave you permission to enter his address book into your computer."

"Actually, that is going to be a surprise Mom and I are giving Dad," Emma explained. "So please don't say anything."

Sam nodded and then pointed to a tree, "What about this one?"

Emma walked around it, looked closely into the tree, and then got on her knees where she checked out the trunk. Sam had picked out a nice straight tree that was thick and tall.

"It's beautiful, Sam!" Emma told him. "I hope when Mom and Dad and I come out here tomorrow, we'll find a tree just like this one."

"I'm sure you will," Sam assured her, pleased she had approved his find.

"Why don't you go find your parents and I'll stay here with the tree," Emma suggested.

Sam nodded and headed off in search of his parents. As Emma gazed at Sam's tree, she wondered what kind of ornaments and lights the Watson's would use.

Seeing Jennifer, Emma yelled, "Hey, Jenn, over here."

Jenn and her family walked up and asked, "Nice tree, is it yours? I didn't see your parents."

"No, my parents aren't here," Emma explained. "I'm here with Sam and his parents."

"Oh, really," Jenn laughed. "Let me guess, you picked it out."

"No, actually Sam did," Emma smiled.

"You did give him your approval, though, right?" Jennifer asked, knowing how Emma picked out her parents' tree every year.

"I helped," Emma admitted, grinning.

"So, did you find your tree yet?" Emma asked Jennifer's boys.

"Not yet," Jonathan answered as he shook his head sadly.

"We want a big one," Jack explained very seriously.

"Well, I happen to know there are bigger ones in the next field over," Emma said as she pointed over the hill. "Tell your dad they have 10-14-foot trees over there."

"Really?" the boys exclaimed excitedly, running off to find their dad.

"Thanks a lot!" Jennifer laughed. "Now I have to go get a bigger tree than I want."

"I don't think so, Jenn," Emma laughed. "I know my trees, but Jenn, I know you, and you have to have the biggest and most expensive one they have on the farm."

Both girls laughed and hugged.

"You're right and now I have to go," Jennifer said as she headed off after her boys.

"Jenn, hold on a minute," Emma said seriously. "I need a favor."

They talked, and then Emma spotted Mary and James coming over.

"Are you sure?" Jennifer asked Emma.

"I am," Emma assured her.

"Okay, I'll see what I can do," Jennifer said, shaking her head.

"Thanks, Jenn, you're the best!" Emma said with a big smile and a hug.

"I will see you later," Jenn waved as she took off to find her boys and her husband.

Emma just smiled and thought, *I am going to have to go see her tree later, for sure. Her tree could make the cover of any magazine. They are always picture perfect.*

"Sam, it's beautiful!" beamed Mary. "James what do you think?"

"Sam, do you have a ladder?" James asked.

"Yes," Sam told his dad.

"Okay, then it's perfect," James agreed.

"Now what do we do?" Mary asked.

"You cut it down," Emma explained.

"Not me," James said vehemently. "It's Sam's tree."

"Okay, I can do this," Sam said, grabbing the saw from his Father.

As he knelt down, Emma knelt down with him, "You want to cut straight across and as close to the bottom as possible. We'll hold the tree so it doesn't fall on you."

"I appreciate that," Sam said as he began sawing.

Before you knew it, they all had to grab hold of it because it was going over.

"Oh, my it's heavy," Mary said. "But it's a beauty."

Once Sam got out from under the tree, Emma couldn't stop laughing.

"What is so funny?" Sam asked.

"You have needles everywhere," Emma said trying to control her laughter. "You might want to brush yourself off."

"Did I get it all?" he asked, turning around so Emma could inspect his clothing.

"You might want to do your back-side," Emma smiled.

"Thank you, I don't want to get needles in my truck," Sam said, brushing off his jeans.

"No, you don't," Emma agreed. "Needles are a lot like sand, you can't ever get rid of them."

The men grabbed the tree and started walking.

Grabbing Emma's arm, Mary said, "I am so glad you joined us today!"

"I am, too," Emma said sincerely. "It's a beautiful tree! I can't wait until my parents and I come out here and get ours."

"When will that be?" Mary asked.

"Tomorrow," Emma explained. "Dad is getting his permanent cast on today."

Just then her phone went off. Looking at it, Emma started to laugh.

"What is so funny?" Mary asked.

"Look," Emma said as she showed Mary the picture Mom had sent her.

"Well, he's in the Christmas spirit," Mary laughed. "You need to show the men."

Emma nodded and when they caught up to Sam and James, she showed it first to James.

Smiling, he said, "I like it."

Sam took a look and said, "Really? A candy cane cast!"

"Yep, I have got to go see this before I head home," Emma laughed.

"I want to see it, too," Mary said, laughing along with Emma.

Frank went in the house and studied his cast, "I like it!"

Ruth could not stop laughing, "I can't believe you asked for a Christmas cast."

"Well, if I am going to wear one, I might as well be festive," Frank said with a big smile.

"Oh, you're festive alright!" Ruth agreed, still laughing.

"You know why I chose these colors don't you?" Frank asked her.

"Yes, Frank, I do. It's one of my favorites, too," she said, kissing her husband. "I'm going to start dinner."

"Can I help?" Frank asked.

"You think you can with that new cast?" Ruth asked him.

"I do have more flexibility now," Frank pointed out.

"Okay, well then, you can set the table," she suggested.

Watching her husband acting more like himself, she said, "Frank, I have to tell you, I am so happy we told Emma the truth and that she is now going to write the Letters."

"I am, too," Frank agreed. "I love you, Ruth, and I'm so sorry for the way I treated you. I promise I will never treat you like that again."

"I know you won't," she smiled.

Glancing out their front window as he was setting the table, Frank said, "Looks like Sam got himself a tree. Do you want to go see it?"

"Why not, and while we are there, let's ask them to join us for dinner," Ruth suggested.

"Great idea," Frank said, grabbing their coats.

"Here, let me help you with that," Frank said, holding the back of her coat for her.

"Oh, thank you," Ruth said with a smile. "You do have more flexibility with that cast."

"It feels great to be able to wiggle my fingers," he laughed.

"Not too heavy?" Ruth asked.

"Not bad, but I have a sling in case my arm gets tired," Frank told her.

Frank and Ruth walked across the street just in time for the unveiling.

Emma waved to her Mom out the window, "Dad, can you get the door for Sam and James?"

"Sure can," Frank said, hurrying to get in front of the guys carrying the heavy tree.

With everybody laughing as Frank made a sweeping gesture with his candy cane cast, Sam and his Dad almost dropped the tree.

"Put it over here," Mary yelled, directing them into the living room where she and Emma had cleared a space for it.

"Hi Ruth, you're just in time," Mary welcomed her. "Your daughter helped us pick out the perfect tree."

"Emma has always had a good eye for trees," Ruth explained. "As a child, she would look for hours before picking out the perfect tree. I didn't mind it when it was a beautiful day like today, but there were some years when it was raining, snowing or just so cold you really didn't care which tree you got."

When the men had the tree in the stand, Sam asked, "Are we ready?"

When his mother nodded, he cut open the net and everyone gazed at the big tree.

"It's beautiful!" Ruth exclaimed.

"It will be even more beautiful when we decorate it," Mary told them. "Sam, where are your decorations?"

"They are still in the attic, Mother," Sam answered. "But I'm hungry. Why don't we go eat then we can come back and decorate?"

"I can definitely eat first," James agreed.

"Ruth would you and Frank like to join us?" Mary invited.

"Actually, I was going to ask you all to join us," Ruth told them. "I put on a roast earlier and it's ready."

"We don't want to impose," Mary said.

"Don't be silly, there's plenty," Ruth assured them. "And James, since I know you like my cherry pie, I made another one this morning."

"Count me in," James said, grabbing everyone's coats.

As they walked to Ruth and Frank's home, Mary said, "Emma, you and Sam did a great job decorating Sam's house."

"Thanks, we had fun!" Emma said with a smile.

"I'm sure you did," Mary said, and both mothers smiled.

During dinner, the Trask and the Watson families talked about Christmas and about how much they had in common.

"Mom, I need to get going," Emma told her once they had cleaned up the dishes. "I still have a lot to do tonight."

"We should get a move on, too," Mary said. "I want to see what kind of decorations my son has."

"I'm not sure he has enough ornaments to fill that big tree," Emma said, knowing there were only a box or two of ornaments still in his attic.

"I'm sure he doesn't," Mary agreed. "That's why I need to know what kind he has so when I go shopping tomorrow, it will all match."

Emma couldn't help but think of Jennifer. Mary will definitely want to go see her tree.

Sam and his parents went back over to his house and started decorating Sam's tree while Emma hung out with her parents for a little while before she went home.

When Emma finally got home, she took off her coat, made herself a cup of hot chocolate, and pulled out her calendar trying to figure out her writing schedule. With her Dad's pen, she filled her calendar and her journal. Then with her Bible in hand, Emma sat in her window seat and prayed that God would give her another task to do for someone before Christmas. As she sat looking out her window, snow flurries started to fall.

"I'm ready, God, let's do this," she said with a smile.

The next morning Emma was pumped, she sprang out of bed and turned up her Christmas music as she got ready for church. Getting into her car, she cranked up her music and sang all the way to church. Looking very closely at the parking lot, Emma paid careful attention to the "puddles," so she would not fall on the patches of light ice from the overnight freeze.

Walking into church, she spotted her parents sitting with Ruth, James, and Sam.

"Hi," she whispered sitting next to Sam.

"You look beautiful," Sam told her.

"Thanks, I made sure I wore the right kind of shoes, though," Emma smiled. "I didn't want to fall on the ice."

Emma smiled as she looked down the row and saw her Dad in his white shirt and emerald sweater which went well with his candy cane cast. As she gazed around the church looking at all the Christmas decorations and white lights, she spotted Jennifer and her family in their usual spot in the second row from the front.

As she listened to the choir's closing song, Emma couldn't help but think that today's message was just for her.

"God bless and have a great week," said her pastor as he dismissed the congregation.

"What did you think of the message?" Sam asked.

Emma did not know how to say how much it spoke directly to her heart. In fact, it confirmed that her Christmas task list was right on target.

"It was great," she told Sam. "Pastor Phil always gives a good message."

"I guess I will see you later," Sam said as his mother reminded Ruth they were going to have dinner together.

Emma said with a smile. "Yes, but first we have to go get our tree!"

"Have fun," Sam said with a smile.

Emma jumped into her car and cranked up her radio as she followed her parents to their home.

"Emma, you might need to cut the tree this year," Dad said. "I'm not sure I can do it with this cast."

"It's okay Dad, I can do it," Emma assured him. "Are you ready, Mom?"

On their way to the farm, Emma turned up the radio.

"I don't think I have ever heard that song before," Ruth commented as she listened to the lyrics.

"Really, Mom?" Emma asked her. "They have been playing it a lot. In fact, every time I get in my car, it comes on."

"It's a beautiful song," Ruth said, thinking how the lyrics reminded her of the Christmas Letters.

"Yes, it is," Emma smiled, thinking about her special Christmas task list.

When they got to the tree farm, Emma said, "Dad, why don't you grab the measuring stick and I will grab a saw."

"I can do that," Frank grinned as he wiggled his fingers.

With it not so cold, the Trask family each wore a light vest with their flannel shirts which suited Frank with his cast. It was hard for him to fit his cast into his heavy winter coat. Emma grabbed the saw and she and her Mom made their way over to Frank who was standing next to another couple talking.

"Hi, we were just admiring your Dad's cast," they smiled.

"It is festive isn't it?" Emma smiled.

"We wish you all a Merry Christmas," they said as they walked away.

"See?" Frank smiled. "Festive!"

"It certainly is!" Ruth laughed.

"Let's grab this wagon," Emma said.

As they all climbed aboard, Emma said, "It isn't as cold as it was yesterday."

"I know, I'm a little disappointed," Ruth said.

"I'm not," Frank said.

"I can see you are enjoying the attention your festive cast is getting," Ruth laughed.

"Well, it's not every day that I can explain the colors of my cast," Frank smiled.

"You have an explanation?" Emma asked as they bumped their way down the road to the field of Christmas trees.

"Sure do," Frank said with certainty. "Do you remember the book, 'The Legend of the Candy Cane'?"[1]

"Yes, of course, you and Mom used to read it to me every Christmas along with the Christmas story," Emma answered. "I have to admit, I had forgotten about it, though. Thanks for reminding me, now I have a new book to add to my collection in my classroom. So, that's why you chose red and white for your cast."

"It is," Frank grinned.

"Very clever, Dad," Emma laughed.

"Ladies and gentlemen, you have arrived," announced their driver. "You all have your tags, saws, and measuring sticks, if you need any help let one of the guys in the field know and they will be glad to help you. I'll be back in a little while to pick you and your tree up."

"Where should we go?" Ruth asked.

"When I was here yesterday, we found Sam's tree the next field over," Emma explained.

"If we can find a tree like Sam's, that would be wonderful," Ruth said with a smile.

"Alright, let's go," Emma said, "Dad, are you coming?"

"I'll catch up," Frank answered.

When Emma looked, Dad was speaking to a young couple with two small children.

Ruth smiled as she watched her husband, "Your Dad loves to talk to people about Christmas."

---

1 https://www.thebettermom.com/blog/2013/12/13/teach-about-jesus-with-the-legend-of-the-candy-cane

Grabbing her Mom's arm, Emma said, "I hope Dad never changes!"

"Me, too!" Ruth agreed with a big smile.

When they reached the next field, Ruth and Emma stopped as they saw Frank was quickly approaching them.

"Why did you to stop?" Frank asked them.

"We wanted to make sure you were still with us," Ruth smiled.

"Of course, I'm with you," Frank smiled at his wife. "Now which tree is ours?"

Scoping out the trees, Emma could see that some of the huge trees that were here yesterday were already gone.

"I hope we can still find one," Emma said. "There doesn't seem to be a lot left."

"Of course, we will," Ruth said. "There are plenty left for us to choose from."

"Let's go this way," Frank suggested as they made their way down a path.

Looking around, he said, "Emma is right, there don't seem to be a lot of huge trees left."

"Where did Mom go?" Emma asked as she could no longer see her.

"You go down this path," Dad said. "I'll make my way up the hill the next path."

Frank and Emma parted ways, looking at trees, but more importantly, looking for Ruth.

"Emma," Ruth called, waving her arms. "Over here, I found our tree."

"Mom, how did you get up here so fast?" Emma asked.

"I knew exactly where I wanted to go and look, I found our tree," Ruth smiled, pointing to a beautiful Cypress pine. "Well, what do you think?"

Emma walked all around the tree, got down on her knees and checked out the trunk. Then she stood up and gazed deeply into the tree.

"Well?" Mom asked again. "What do you think?"

Smiling, Emma told her, "You found it! I don't remember seeing this tree yesterday, though, we must have walked this field ten times!"

"Go find your Dad," Ruth said. "I'll stay by the tree."

"No need," Frank said as he approached them.

Turning around seeing her Dad, Emma asked, "How did you find us?"

"How could I miss you with your bright red vest?" Frank laughed.

"I love this vest," Emma grinned.

"So, Frank, what do you think?" Ruth asked.

"If Emma says it's okay, it's fine with me," Frank agreed.

"It's perfect! Now for the fun part," Emma said, bending down on her knees and scooting herself under the tree. "Can you hand me the saw?"

Handing her daughter, the saw, Ruth said, "Here you go. Be careful!"

Emma sawed until the tree started to sway, then she yelled, "Grab hold, I don't want it falling on me!"

Frank grabbed for the tree with his left hand, but missed and the tree came down on Emma.

"Emma, are you alright?" he yelled.

"I'm fine, but can you please get the tree off of me?" she yelled, her voice muffled beneath the huge trees branches.

Frank grabbed a hold of the middle of the tree and he and Ruth pulled up enough for Emma to climb out.

Standing up, Emma looked at her parents, "That was fun!"

"I'm sorry, Emma, it slipped. I'm not used to reaching with my left hand," Frank said. "I have a good hold now."

"Me, too!" Ruth said as they both started laughing.

"What are you laughing at?" Emma asked.

Ruth and Frank laughed even harder.

Emma grabbed a hold of the back of the tree and they all made their way down the hill carrying the ten-foot tree. It was a little slenderer than Sam's tree which was exactly the way Ruth liked her tree. Dropping their tree by the side of the road and waiting for the wagon, Emma could see people around her looking in their direction.

"Dad, you're gaining attention with the cast again," Emma told him.

"I don't think they're looking at me," Frank laughed.

"Of course, they are," Emma said.

"No, Emma," Mom said as she walked over and whispered, "They are staring at you, my dear."

"Me?"

"Emma, you are covered with sap and needles," Ruth laughed. "You look like a tree."

Emma hadn't really brushed herself when she climbed out from under the tree. She was focused on the mud that she was laying in. Since the weather was warmer, the snow had melted. Now she was covered in mud, sap, and needles.

"That's what Sam looked like yesterday," she laughed remembering the picture he made.

"You'll need a bath when you get to the house," Ruth told her.

"I didn't bring extra clothes," Emma said, shaking the needles out of her hair.

"Let's stop by your house first so you can clean up, then we'll go home," Ruth suggested.

The wagon pulled up, the driver jumped down and took one look at Emma, "Did you have fun?"

Smiling back, Emma said, "We did. It is a family tradition that I chop down the tree."

"It looks like the tree almost won, though," he said laughing.

Everyone laughed, including Emma.

"All aboard!" he yelled and the wagon made its way back to the parking lot, where a couple of workers shook, netted, and placed their tree on top of Emma's car.

With all of them in Emma's car, Emma got a real look at herself in the mirror.

"Lovely," she said with a smile.

Frank turned up the music and they sang all the way to Emma's house.

While Emma was cleaning up, Frank saw his pen on her desk.

Ruth saw him picking it up and asked, "Frank, are you alright?"

"Yes," he said turning to look at her. "I was just thinking how proud I am of Emma that she is going to use this. It's such a beautiful pen!"

"It sure is!" Ruth agreed.

Seeing Frank's address book and the labels on the corner of the desk, Ruth suggested to Frank, "Would you grab us a couple of waters from Emma's kitchen?"

Ruth managed to hide the address book and labels as Frank made his way into the kitchen.

Coming out of her room, Emma noticed what Mom was doing and asked, "Shall we go and set your tree up?"

After Emma pulled into her parents' drive, she went over to Sam's to see if he and his Dad could help them get their tree off the car and into the stand in their living room.

"Did you find a tree?" Sam asked when he answered the door.

"Yes, we did," Emma said with a smile. "Can you and your Dad help us out?"

"I can, but Mother and Father went to town, Mother needed more ornaments," Sam said with a smile.

Peaking around Sam, Emma agreed, "Yep, your tree still needs more ornaments."

Grabbing his coat, Sam and Emma made their way over to her parents' home.

"Hi, Frank," Sam said. "Need a hand?"

"Yes, thanks," Frank answered. "Can you grab my ladder and we'll have this tree into the living room in no time."

Sam made his way into their garage and grabbed the ladder. Emma and Ruth made the room ready for the men to bring in their tree.

"I think this tree is as big as mine!" Sam exclaimed as he helped Frank lift it off Emma's car and bring it in the front door.

"It is, but not as wide," Ruth agreed. "The tree stand is over there. Just a little more to the left and back a little more. That's perfect."

Cutting the net, the tree sprang into shape.

"It's a beautiful tree, Mom," Emma said smiling.

"Yes, it is, Ruth," Frank beamed. "You found our perfect tree."

"Well, it wasn't that hard, I just walked up the hill and it practically jumped out in front of me," Ruth explained. "In fact, I tripped over a stump and the tree caught my balance."

"Well, it's a beauty, but I really need to get going," Emma told them.

"Emma, I didn't get a chance to make you something to eat," Ruth said.

"It's okay, Mom. I'll grab something on the way home," Emma assured her.

"I better be going, too," Sam said.

"Thanks for your help, Sam," Frank said.

As Sam and Emma walked outside, Sam asked, "What are you doing for dinner?"

"I don't know yet, but I'll come up with something," Emma answered.

Rubbing his hands together because the temperature had dropped, Sam said, "I haven't eaten yet, so I was wondering if you would like to go to dinner?"

"I would, but I have way too much to do," Emma said walking to her car. "On second thought, I'll buy us a pizza if you come over and help with Dad's address book."

"Double pepperoni and cheese?" Sam asked.

"Sure, why not," Emma said, laughing.

"I'll just leave my parents a note and I'll be right over," Sam said as he headed into his house.

Turning up her radio, Emma made her way home singing Christmas carols. Once she got home, she quickly cleaned up her living room, and ordered a double pepperoni cheese pizza.

It didn't take long for Sam to knock on her door, "You're just in time, the pizza just got here."

"That was quick," he said taking his coat off. "It's getting colder out there! I think I heard that we could even get a couple of inches of snow tonight."

"That would be nice, but I have learned that when the weatherman says a lot of snow their prediction is always wrong and when they predict less than an inch we get three or more inches of snow," Emma warned him.

"Three weeks to go until Christmas," Sam said. "Are you ready?"

"Not really, that is why I can't thank you enough for offering to help me with this is," she said as she tossed him her Dad's address book.

"Glad to help," Sam said as he sat down at her computer.

After handing him a plate with two pieces of pizza and a glass of Sprite, Emma made her way over to her kitchen table and glanced down at a blank piece of paper.

"How many letters do you still need to write?" Sam asked her.

"Six," Emma answered.

"That doesn't sound that bad," Sam said.

"No, but each one takes time," Emma told him. "Can you please pass me your grandfather's pen?"

Picking up the box and opening it, Sam said, "I never get tired of looking at it."

"I know what you mean," Emma agreed. "It's very unusual and light which makes writing with it a lot easier. It's like the words just flow from the pen onto the paper."

Sam and Emma worked quietly for a couple of hours. After a while, Sam leaned back in the computer chair, lifting his hands up above his head and stretching.

"Done?" she asked.

"Not quite, but I need a break," Sam answered, standing up. "Your Dad knows a lot of people!"

"He does and he meets new people every day," Emma said smiling. "I would not be surprised if he has some new names already. Like today when we reached the tree farm, Mom and I saw Dad speaking to a young couple with young kids. Dad was showing the children his cast. I will bet you that not only did Dad get their names and address so he could keep in touch, he told those kids about the 'Legend of the Candy Cane.'"

"You can't be serious," Sam said, shaking his head.

"I am," Emma grinned.

"How do you know what he said to them?" Sam asked.

"I know my Dad and he was showing them his cast," Emma explained. "And his cast looks like a candy cane."

"What is the 'Legend of the Candy Cane?'" he asked.

"Well, it's a great story that my parents would read to me when I was a child every Christmas," Emma explained.

"Tell me," he asked, as he sat back down at the computer.

"Not tonight, we have work to do," Emma said shaking her head. "Look it up and read the story, I promise you won't be disappointed. Now, I need to get back to work."

Emma laid the pen down and reread her letter. When she felt she was finished with it, she folded it neatly, placed it in its envelope, and sealed it. She addressed it and put a stamp on it and added it to the pile she had completed.

Three more to go, she said to herself as she looked at the clock. It had taken her close to three hours to write three letters.

Sam stopped soon after and got up to stretch, "I think I made some headway."

Getting up herself, Emma said, "Sam, thanks again, you have no idea how much I appreciate the help."

"You're welcome," he said grabbing his coat. "I need to get going, though. My parents will begin to wonder why it took so long for us to eat dinner."

"Drive safe and I'll see you tomorrow," Emma said.

"Not if we get the snow they are predicting," Sam said shaking his head.

"Oh, I'll see you tomorrow, Sam," Emma assured him.

"Where do you think he is?" Mary asked her husband, looking out the window at the falling snow.

"I'm sure he and Emma are just fine," James said not looking up from his book.

"But it has been three hours," Mary pointed out. "It does not take three hours to eat dinner."

"What are you worried about?" James said with a smile. "I thought you liked Emma."

"I do, I was just hoping they would both come back here after they ate and help me finish decorating the tree," Mary said, looking out the window for the hundredth time.

Putting down his book, James asked, "You want help with the tree?"

"I value Emma's opinion and I need Sam to reach the top of the tree," Mary explained.

Smiling broadly and getting up from the couch, James said, "You must really like her. You never ask for help. In fact, you always insist on doing it yourself."

"Well, I do like her," Mary agreed. "More importantly Sam likes her, too."

"Now, Mary, they're friends," James pointed out seeing where his wife was going with this.

"I know, but a mother can always hope," she said with a smile.

Hearing the garage door open, James said, "There he is now."

"Hi, did you have fun?" Mary asked, as Sam walked in the door.

"Yes, but my neck and back are killing me," Sam answered.

"What?" Mary said looking puzzled.

"Relax, Mother, Emma wrote three of her letters and I entered addresses into her computer from Frank's address book," Sam explained, laughing at his mother's expression.

"How far did you get?" James asked.

"We made progress," Sam answered.

Looking over at the tree, he said, "Mother, the tree looks great, but you missed a spot right here."

Smiling at her, he said, "I'm off to bed, we have a busy day at school tomorrow. What are you two up to tomorrow?"

"I'll do whatever your mother asks me to do. She's in charge of our social calendar," James said as he picked up his book again.

Chapter 15

Early the next morning, Emma turned over and turned off her alarm clock. *It can't be time to get up already,* she thought. *I just went bed*! Emma had set her clock an hour earlier, so she could add some more names from her dad's address book into her computer. She slowly got out of bed and made her way into the kitchen where she made herself a cup of coffee. She noticed that the light from outside was brighter than normal. Opening her blinds, she could not believe her eyes.

Her phone rang, "Hello?"

"No school today," Jenn told her.

"I figured as much," Emma said smiling as she made her way to her window seat. "Go back to bed, Jenn, I'll call you later."

Looking outside, there appeared to be over four inches of fresh snow. *It looks like the weatherman was right this time. I should have checked the weather report last night*, she said to herself as she sipped her coffee.

Emma sat in her window seat for a while that morning writing in her journal and thinking about her day. Then she got up and made her way to her computer. Having the day off from school would allow her to get a lot done on Dad's address list and hopefully finish the Christmas Letters.

It was noon when Emma decided to take a break and call her parents.

"Good morning, Emma," Ruth said. "Did you go back to sleep once you knew there was no school?"

"No, I was already up," Emma told her. "I wanted to get some things done today before school."

"Have you been working on the letters or addresses this morning?" Ruth asked.

"Both," Emma told her Mom. "I'm hoping to have the three remaining letters and the address book finished today."

"That would be wonderful, your Dad will be pleased," Ruth told her daughter.

"Yes, but remember, Mom, no word about his address book," Emma reminded her. "I would like that to be a surprise for Christmas."

"I understand," Mom assured her. "Not a word."

"What's Dad doing?" Emma asked.

"He's about to go outside?" Ruth told her waving to Frank as he zipped up his coat and headed out the door.

"Why?" Emma asked,

"Because Sam is going to clean our driveway for us," Ruth explained.

"That's nice of him," Emma said with a smile.

"I thought so," Ruth agreed. "That way I don't have to do it."

"Tell Dad to be careful," Emma added. "We don't want another accident."

"I will," Ruth assured her. "I better get outside to see if they need any help. Enjoy your day off, Emma."

"I will, Mom, you, too," Emma said as she hung up.

I guess I ought to do my driveway, too, she said to herself looking outside. *But I really don't want to.*

Instead, she sat down at her table and stared at a piece of paper. After thirty minutes, no words came to mind. *I have nothing, Mrs. White, I'm sorry, I guess your letter is going to have to wait.*

Deciding she might as well tackle her driveway, Emma grabbed her boots, coat, and gloves and went to her garage where she pulled out her new snow blower. *You should work*, she said to it. *Dad checked you out last week*. She turned the knob and pulled the string and it started right up. Due to the brightness of the snow and the sun, Emma grabbed her sunglasses out of the car. She started down her driveway, row by row and when she was done, she stopped and admired her work.

Emma noticed Mrs. Tracey, her elderly widowed neighbor, trying to shovel her own driveway. Emma walked her snow blower across the street.

"Good morning, Mrs. Tracey," Emma greeted her. "This snow is wet and heavy, so I thought I could give you a hand with my snow blower."

"Are you sure?" Mrs. Tracey said, looking relieved.

"I'm sure," Emma said with a smile. "It shouldn't take too long."

"Okay, then when you're done, come on into the house and I'll fix us some hot chocolate," Mrs. Tracey told her.

"That's not necessary," Emma assured her.

"I want, too, now you remove this stuff and come inside when you're done," Mrs. Tracey told her firmly.

"Yes, Mam," Emma smiled.

What a lady! Emma thought as she quickly started up her snow blower and set to work clearing the sidewalk, driveway, and walkway to Mrs. Tracey's front door. *Smart as a tack!* Emma knew she had been a History teacher for thirty years at the high school. *I do not have time for hot chocolate with Mrs. Tracey*, Emma thought. She would be here longer than she wanted, but she knew that since Mr. Tracey died, Mrs. Tracey really didn't have anybody to talk to.

Her son came over when he could, but being an airline pilot, he was gone quite a bit. Emma had taken upon herself to check in with Mrs. Tracey once in a while to see how she was doing.

Looking at her watch, she thought, *that took longer than I thought, but who cares.* Emma was enjoying herself despite being half frozen. Clearing off the steps, Emma knocked on the door.

"Are you done?" Mrs. Tracey called.

"I am," Emma replied.

"Great job!" Mrs. Tracey told her. "You deserve a cup of hot chocolate, but please take off your boots. I don't want snow all over my floor."

"Yes, Ms. Tracey," Emma said as she removed her gloves, sunglasses, coat, and boots.

Rubbing her hands together, Emma made her way into her kitchen and sat down at the table where she found a plate of chocolate chip muffins and a Christmas mug of hot chocolate.

"Mrs. Tracey, how did you know chocolate chip muffins are my favorite?" she asked.

"I called your Mom this morning and asked," Mrs. Tracey admitted.

"How did you know I would be over today?" Emma asked.

"I knew you would eventually come out and clear your driveway," Mrs. Tracey said with a guilty little smile.

"So, you waited until you saw me out there and then you came out knowing I would see you trying to shovel yours," Emma surmised.

Laughing, Mrs. Tracey admitted, "I sure did and it worked, too!"

"Mrs. Tracey, I'm speechless!" Emma said laughing.

"Good, then I can do the talking," Mrs. Tracey smiled and took a sip of her hot chocolate. "Dig in girl!"

Emma took a muffin and began to eat. In fact, she inhaled the entire muffin in no time, "These are delicious, I haven't eaten anything since breakfast."

"You may have another," Mrs. Tracey said, offering her the plate.

"Okay, I will," Emma said, taking another of Mrs. Tracey's delicious muffins. "So, what did you want to talk to me about Mrs. Tracey?"

"I wanted to let you know how proud I am of you for writing your Dad's Christmas Letters this year," she said sincerely.

"How did you know?" Emma asked.

"Your Mom told me," Mrs. Tracey said. "She also said that you were entering your Dad's address book into your computer."

"Yes, I am," Emma told her. "I am planning on giving that to Dad for Christmas."

"I hope that is not his only Christmas present," Mrs. Tracey said.

"No, just part of it," Emma assured her.

"Well, that's good because if that was the only thing you were giving your Dad for Christmas, you and I would be having another talk," Mrs. Tracey said with a smile.

"I'm definitely getting something else for Dad, I just haven't figured out what yet," Emma told her. "Shopping for Mom is easy, but Dad is another story."

"Speaking of Christmas shopping, Emma, I need a favor," Mrs. Tracey said. "Would you have time to take me shopping for my family?"

Looking surprised, she said, "Mrs. Tracey, I would love to, but I have so much on my plate already. I will have to look at my calendar and get back to you."

Looking into Mrs. Tracey's eyes, Emma could see her disappointment.

"I understand," Mrs. Tracey said. "I will get my son to help me."

"When does he get back into town?" she asked.

"The end of next week," Mrs. Tracey told her.

"That only gives you one week to get your shopping done," Emma said, shaking her head.

"Oh, I can do it, I've done it before," Mrs. Tracey assured her. "Don't give it another thought, now have another muffin."

As Mrs. Tracey got up to get them more hot chocolate, Emma felt a tug on her heart. She knew that this was the task she was being given to do.

"Mrs. Tracey, I looked at my calendar, would next Saturday work for you to go shopping?" Emma asked, getting up and helping Ms. Tracey pour the hot chocolate.

"Saturday?" Mrs. Tracey asked. "You have too much to do, Emma. It's okay, really."

"I can manage and besides I haven't finished all of my shopping yet either," Emma told her. "So, how about it?"

"Are you sure, Emma?" Mrs. Tracey asked.

"I'm sure, Mrs. Tracey," Emma assured her neighbor. "Now let's sit and finish our hot chocolate before it gets cold."

Emma smiled as she took a bite of the warm muffin and thought to herself, *I can do this*.

Once Emma helped Mrs. Tracey clean off her table and washed the dishes they used, Emma got ready to head back to her house. Putting on her sunglasses, Emma looked toward the sun and could feel its warmth on her face. Taking a deep breath, she put on her gloves, walked down the steps, and pulled her snow blower behind her. Putting it in her garage, she picked up a plastic cup and reached into the bag of sand that her Dad bought for her. Emma sprinkled sand onto her driveway and up her front steps just in case the slush on her driveway became an ice rink. Then she went over to Mrs. Tracey's house and sprinkled sand on her sidewalk and steps as well.

Before going into her house, Emma put her sunglasses back in her car and took off her gloves and boots. Exhausted from snow plowing and her stomach full of muffins and hot chocolate, Emma felt sleepy. Before she took a nap, she checked her phone and found that she had a couple of messages. One was from Sam and one from her Mom.

She texted Sam and told him she had been out shoveling and now she was going to rest. Making her way into her bedroom, Emma called her Mom and got the answering machine. She told her Mrs. Tracey sends her love and that she was going to take a nap. As Emma laid her head onto her pillow and pulled up her flannel sheets, a smile came over her face and she closed her eyes.

Emma woke with a start, looked at the clock, and realized it was five o clock. She headed into her kitchen and made herself something to eat. Feeling refreshed, Emma began Mrs. White's letter and by ten o'clock she had finished all the letters and all the addresses were in her computer. All I have to do is print the labels out and give them to Dad at Christmas.

Emma got up from her desk and made herself a cup of hot chocolate. She grabbed her coat and walked outside to her front porch. Emma wrapped her hands around her favorite Christmas mug and took a deep breath.

God, thank You so much for snow and Mrs. Tracey.

Light snow was falling and with the street so quiet, she could actually hear the snow coming down like tiny pieces of ice. With the moon shining on the snow, it glistened. Emma stood outside longer than she thought she had, but it was well worth it.

Mrs. White and Mr. Jones, I hope you enjoy your Christmas Letters, she thought.

"No answer?" Mary asked Sam.

"No, Mother," Sam said shaking his head. "She must have her phone off."

He thinks Emma is avoiding him, Mary thought to herself, looking at the expression on her son's face.

"Ruth said she was going out to shovel snow earlier," Mary reminded him.

"Yes, I know but I have not heard from her all afternoon," Sam said, obviously concerned he had not heard from her all day.

"I think you're getting worried for nothing," James said.

"Father, Emma always answers her phone," Sam explained.

"Well, maybe she's working on her letters or the address labels?" James suggested.

"She always answers my text and quickly I might add," Sam said. "You and Father going to be alright if I run over there and check on her?"

"We'll be fine," Mary assured him. "We're not going out."

As Sam was about to walk out the door, Emma texted, "I'm fine, it's been a busy day. See you tomorrow."

"There, she answered you," Mary said.

"Yes," Sam said.

"You sound disappointed," Mary observed.

"No, I'm glad she's alright," Sam said, but his mother could tell what her son wanted.

"Well, it's getting late, I'm off to bed," Mary said. "James are you coming?"

"I'll be there soon," he assured her, knowing what she wanted him to do.

"Sam, what's wrong?" James asked his son. "Is there a problem at the school?"

"No," Sam answered. "Jennifer called and asked me to go in early tomorrow and make sure the heat is working properly throughout the building and that the parking lot has been cleared."

"Then what is it?" James asked, knowing something was definitely bothering Sam.

"As each day gets closer to Christmas, it reminds me that once the Christmas break is over, I won't be back," Sam told his father, shaking his head.

"That is what you wanted, isn't it?" James asked.

"It was and I guess it still is, but I am going to miss working at the school," Sam admitted.

"You mean you're going to miss Emma," James said with a smile.

"Yes, and Jennifer, and the rest of the teachers, and Ruth. Everybody is so nice and we all get along so well," Sam said. "Jennifer and I make a great team. I'm not sure I am going to have that at the high school, especially since I am going to be the one in charge."

"I remember when you started this job you couldn't wait until Christmas so you would be out of the elementary school," James commented. "Now you don't want to leave?"

"I do and then I don't," Sam said, sounding confused. "I just don't know, anymore. I have been waiting for the new high school to open and now that it is, I don't know if I want the job anymore."

"Well, you only have a couple more weeks, so the best thing you can do is to pray," James advised him. "Pray about what God wants you to do next."

"I have been and so far, He hasn't answered," Sam told him.

"Sam, the answer will come, but you have to be patient," James told him.

"I have been, believe me," Sam said, shaking his head.

Getting up, James said, "The answers will come, I promise. Good night, son."

"Night, Dad," Sam said as he made his way out to his front porch and stared up into the night sky.

Okay, God, I need answers, he said quietly.

The next few weeks of school, Emma rose up early enough to pick up her Mom every morning. Emma had a list of things to do and time was running out before the Christmas break. Emma could not be happier, though, except knowing Sam was leaving made her a little sad.

At lunch, Emma told Ruth about the next couple of Christmas tasks God had given her.

"I think that's a great idea, but can we pull it off?" Ruth asked her.

"Mom, we pulled off a baby shower in three days for Stacey, I think we can handle a staff Christmas party, but we are going to have to get help," Emma told her. "I have already spoke to the teachers and they are all in. We have even decided what we are getting Sam and Jennifer for Christmas."

"What?" Ruth asked.

After Emma told her Mom the news, Ruth said, "Jenn and Sam are going to love their gifts."

"I certainly hope so," Emma said with a smile.

When Emma got home after dropping her Mom off, she sat in her window seat with her calendar and journal and checked off another task God had given her. Tomorrow was going to be an awesome day.

Picking up her phone, Emma called Jennifer to let her know about the party.

"We can't have the party tomorrow," Jennifer said. "There is not enough time!"

"Jenn, I've got this and the staff already knows," Emma assured her. "Now can I please speak to Jason?"

"Sure, but why?" Jennifer asked.

"Jenn, it's Christmas, put Jason on," Emma insisted.

"Okay," Jennifer said.

Hearing all the commotion in the background, Emma knew she had the perfect gift for Jennifer.

"Hello! Jason, it's Emma," she said. "I need a favor."

Emma told him about the staff party and what she had planned for Jennifer.

"Are you sure you want to do this?" Jason asked her.

"I'm sure, as long as it is okay with you," Emma said.

"Yes, in fact your timing could not be better!" Jason told Emma. "Thank you, she's going to love it."

"I'm glad!" Emma said excitedly. "Now remember four o'clock tomorrow."

"I won't forget," Jason assured her. "I'll have everything ready."

"Great!" Emma said. "I'll see you tomorrow."

Hanging up the phone, Emma smiled and made her next call to Sam.

"Hi, Sam, we are all set for tomorrow," she told him. "Did you get everything that I asked you for?"

"Yes, I did," Sam assured her.

"Thanks, Sam, I can't thank you enough," Emma said.

"You can thank me by having dinner with me," Sam said.

"Sure, I'll be ready in an hour," Emma agreed.

"Do you want me to pick you up or are you coming over to your Mom's?" Sam asked.

"No, you can pick me up," Emma answered. "I'll see you in an hour, Sam."

"Great, see you then," Sam said with a smile.

"Who was that?" Mary asked him.

"It was Emma, we're going to dinner," Sam told her.

"Then you better change," she suggested.

"What is wrong with what I'm wearing?" Sam asked her.

"James, tell him," Mary said.

"Son, do what your Mother says," not looking up from his book.

"How's this?" Sam asked a few minutes later coming out from his bedroom.

"Better, just let me fix your collar," Mary said.

"Mother, really?" Sam laughed.

"Hold still," she said fixing the back of his collar. "You look handsome!"

"I love you, too, Mother," he said as she kissed him on the cheek. "I'll see you both later."

"Have fun!" Mary called and then watched her son pull away and looked up and smiled.

"You have this, right?" Mary asked.

"Have what?" James asked, thinking she was talking to him.

"Nothing, put that book down and let's get some dinner," Mary told him walking into the kitchen.

"Yes, Mary," James said with a knowing smile.

Emma turned up the Christmas music and changed clothes at least three times before she had the perfect outfit. Sitting in her window seat, she waited and waited and when she was about to call, Sam pulled up.

"Sorry, I'm late," Sam apologized. "Mother made me change my clothes, how do I look?"

Laughing, Emma said, "You look very nice!"

"So, do you," Sam told her with a smile. "Shall we go? I was thinking after dinner we can drive around town and check out the Christmas lights."

"That sounds like fun," Emma said with a smile. "I've been so busy I haven't had the chance to do that."

"Great, so where should we go to eat?" Sam asked her.

"How about the diner?" Emma suggested. "I am in the mood for chili, if you don't mind?"

"You want chili?" Sam asked her.

"Yes, it's cold, I'm starving, and I really don't want to wait an hour or two to eat," Emma told him.

"The diner it is," Sam said.

It was not very crowded, so they were eating and talking about the staff Christmas party in no time.

"That is quite a gift," Sam said after Emma told him what they were getting for Jennifer for Christmas. "Jennifer is going to love it and so is her husband. She deserves it, she has been a great boss. I wish I could take her with me."

"No, you don't!" Emma told him emphatically.

"Why not?" Sam asked.

"Jennifer would have to report to you and that she would not like," Emma told him. "She likes being the boss."

Laughing, Sam said, "You right about that!"

"Very bad idea!" Emma said firmly.

"Well, I just hope I find an Assistant Principal that knows what they are doing and we get along like the staff here," Sam stated.

"Are you getting excited about being the Principal?" Emma asked him.

"Yes and no," Sam said, shaking his head. "Jennifer, your Mom, and the staff have been great. I would love to take all of them with me."

"I get it, but you can't have us," Emma told him.

"Are you sure you want to stay with Kindergarten and not work with High School students?" Sam asked her.

"I'm sure," Emma answered. "I love seeing the transformation the kids make from the first day of school until the last. They grow and change so much. It's hard to believe sometimes. I have seen the shyest child come in and by the last day of school, they are the leaders of the class. I have also seen the ones who can barely read, begin to read like a first or second grader. I think that is my favorite part, seeing these kids really excel in school. That is why I love teaching and hanging in my classroom; I see so much."

"I can understand that," Sam agreed. "I also think we will be surprised on how much some of the boys and girls have grown during the Christmas break."

"You won't be there, though," Emma reminded him.

"No, but I will stop by when I can to check up on everyone," Sam promised.

"That would be nice," Emma said. "You are going to be missed, especially your cookies. I hope you remember you are bringing cookies tomorrow for the party."

"Of course," Sam assured her. "Now, are you ready to go and look at some lights?"

"I am," Emma said. "We do have a big day tomorrow, so we can't take too long, though."

"Yes, it is," Sam agreed.

"I'm so excited," Emma said. "I can't wait!"

"Good morning, Emma," Ruth greeted her. "Did you sleep well?"

"Not really," Emma said. "I am too excited!"

"About your date last night or the party?" Ruth asked.

"The party and it wasn't a date," Emma told her, surprised she knew she had gone out with Sam.

"You had fun, though?" Ruth asked her.

"Yes, Mom, we had fun," Emma answered her.

"You would have liked it to be a date, though, right?" Ruth asked.

"Mom, you know the rules, no dating co-workers," Emma reminded her. "Besides, I'm not sure I want to date Sam. We have a good friendship and I don't want to ruin it."

"I get it, but you can't live in fear," Ruth told her. "Love is messy."

"Who said anything about love?" Emma asked. "Can we please talk about something else?"

"Yes, did you talk to Jason?" Ruth asked.

"Yes, it's all set, he'll be here at four," Emma assured her.

"Emma, it's quite a gift. Jennifer is going to love it," Ruth said.

"I know, I can't wait to see her face!" Emma said excitedly.

"Me neither!" Ruth agreed.

Emma and Ruth sang Christmas songs all the way to school.

The morning went by quickly, Emma entered test scores and her kids watched movies all morning. At lunch, Emma and Ruth joined the other teachers and staff to set up the large conference room for the party. When the day was over, all the teachers and staff brought in their food and gifts for each other. With the party going strong and Jennifer giving her gifts to the staff and to Sam and Ruth, Emma received a text saying Jason was there.

"Ladies and Gentlemen, can you all take your seats. Jennifer please come up here," Emma announced.

"What have you done?" Jennifer asked suspiciously.

"Jenn, you are the best principal we can ask for and we thank you for all that you do. This is for you," Emma said, handing Jennifer an envelope.

Emma could not hold back her tears, she loved her friend and she knew she deserved it.

"Are you kidding me?" Jennifer yelled.

"Jason, boys, come on in," Emma called out.

Jason came in holding a dozen red roses for his wife.

"What is it?" a new teacher yelled.

Holding back her tears, Jennifer said, "My husband and I are going away for the weekend and Emma is watching my boys."

Everybody applauded.

"When do you leave?" another teacher asked.

"Right now!" Jason announced, looking at his wife. "Your bags are packed and we are out of here."

Hugging her friend, Jennifer said, "I don't know what to say!"

"Kiss your boy's goodbye and take off," Emma told her with a big smile.

"Are you sure?" Jennifer asked.

"My brother is coming over, so the boys and I are spending the night at Mom's tomorrow," Emma explained.

"Thank you, Emma," Jennifer said with tears in her eyes.

"Now get out of here," Emma said, and everybody walked them out and cheered as they drove off.

"Miss Emma, we're staying with you?" Jack, Jennifer's oldest son asked her.

"Yes, can you believe it?" Emma smiled at them. "We finally get to have a sleep over and tomorrow, we're going to my mom's because Ben and the boys are coming. And do you know what? We all get to sleep there tomorrow!"

"Yes," the Jonathan cheered. "Can we go now?"

"Not quite yet, we need to clean up first," Emma said. "Can you help me?"

"Sure, the faster we get done, the faster we can go!" Jack agreed.

They all cleaned, so it did not take very long until they were done.

"Sam, thank you so much for all of your help," Emma told him as they took care of the last bag of garbage.

"You're welcome and thank you for the mixer" he smiled, wanting to say more, but it didn't seem like the right time.

"You deserve it! Why don't you and your parents join us for dinner tomorrow night?" Emma asked him. "Ben and the boys are coming over, so it will be a lot of fun!"

"Are you sure it's okay with your Mom?" Sam asked.

"I'm sure!" Emma assured him.

"Well then, I'll check with Mother and Father, but I'm sure it's okay," Sam told her.

Putting the last of the chairs up, he asked her, "Do the boys like s'mores?"

"Why don't you ask them?" Emma suggested. "They're over there with Mom."

"Emma, great party," the staff all said as they headed out.

"Thanks, you all have a great Christmas and stay safe," Emma told them. "See you all next year!"

Emma, the boys, Ruth, and Sam made their way out to the parking lot.

"Well, Mom, we did it," Emma said with a big grin. "Thanks again for everything."

"Emma, you did most of the work, I'm so proud of you, and I love my gift," Ruth told her

"I thought you might," Emma said.

"Jennifer did great, didn't she?" Ruth asked.

"Yes, she did!" Emma agreed, holding up her own gift.

"Okay, boys, get into the car," Emma told them. "Mom, we'll see you tomorrow afternoon, okay?"

"That will be fine," Ruth said. "See you then."

Getting into her car, she turned to the boys and said, "Well guys, are you ready to party?"

She turned up the radio and they all sang Christmas carols as they made their way to Emma's house where they ordered pizza and watched movies until the boys fell asleep on her living room floor.

Early the next morning, Emma was awakened by her phone ringing, "Hello? Yes, this is she. What? A girl! That's wonderful! How is Stacey doing? Great! Please tell her congratulations for me and tell her I'll come by tomorrow. Today? Okay," getting up and keeping an eye on the boys who were still sleeping. "How about I come by this afternoon? Good, I'll see you then and thank you for calling."

"Miss Emma, who was that?" Jack asked her, rubbing the sleep out of his eyes.

"That was a mom who just told me that her daughter had a baby girl," Emma told him. "We all thought she was going to have a boy, but apparently God chose to give them a girl instead."

While the boys watched TV, Emma made her way to her window seat and wrote in her journal, and watched the light snow begin to fall.

"It looks like we're getting more snow," she told them.

The boys cheered.

"When are we going to Miss Ruth's?" Jonathan asked her.

"Right after you finish breakfast if you want."

"So, when you're done, please go brush your teeth and get dressed," Emma told them.

Emma could not believe how well Jennifer's boys behaved and obeyed, but then again, having Jennifer as their mom, Emma should have known better.

Climbing into Emma's car, Jack asked, "Miss Emma, can you turn the music up again?"

"Sure," Emma answered, and they sang Christmas songs all the way to Ruth's house.

As Emma turned in her parents' driveway, she looked across the street to see Sam and his Dad working on Sam's new snow blower. Emma waved and made her way into her parents' home with Jennifer's boys.

"Hello?" she called.

"We're in here," Ruth answered. "Emma, we weren't expecting to see you guys until later this afternoon."

"I know, but I got a call very early this morning and I was so excited I couldn't go back to sleep, guess what?" Emma said excitedly.

"What?" Ruth asked.

"Stacey had her baby!" Emma announced.

"She did?" Ruth asked. "That's great! How is he doing and what's his name?"

"Mom, she had a girl!" Emma said laughing.

"A girl?" Ruth asked. "I thought she was having a boy?"

"We all did," Emma agreed. "But you know God."

"Yes, I do!" Ruth said with a smile. "How is she?"

"She is seven pounds, eleven inches long, healthy, and Stacey is doing great, too," Emma told Ruth. "She did have a C-section, though, but everything went great. She wants us to come by this afternoon. Do you think Dad can handle the boys for a little while?"

"I'm sure he'll be fine," Ruth assured her. "Ben and Cathy will be here with the boys early this afternoon."

"Then why don't we head on over after lunch?" Emma suggested.

"Sounds good," Ruth agreed.

"Where's Dad?" Emma asked.

"In his office," Ruth answered.

"Okay if I go say hi?" Emma asked her Mom.

"Sure, I'll go check on the boys," Ruth said.

Walking down to her Dad's office, Emma knocked.

"Yes?" her Dad asked. "Emma, I didn't hear you come in, what are you doing here so early?"

"I brought the boys so they can build a snowman with you," Emma told him.

Looking outside, Frank could see the snow coming down.

"I'm kidding, Dad," Emma said. "I really came to tell you Josh's mom, Stacey, had a baby girl last night."

"I thought she was having a boy?" Frank said.

"Stacey prayed for a girl and God answered her even when the doctors told her she was going to have a boy!" Emma said with a smile.

"I bet she's thrilled," Frank smiled.

"Mom and I are going over this afternoon if you don't mind watching the boys while we're gone," Emma said. "Mom says Ben and Cathy will be here later with their boys if you need any help."

"We'll be fine, give Stacey our best," Frank told her. "Emma, please close the door and sit down for a minute, though."

"What's wrong?" she asked.

"Nothing, I just want to talk to you a minute," Frank said. "I got another call yesterday from Mrs. White. She told me to tell you thank you for the letter."

"Really?" Emma asked.

"You sound surprised," her dad said.

"I am, I had a hard time with Mrs. White's letter," Emma confessed. "The words did not come as easy as some of the others. In fact, I think her letter was the hardest."

"Sometimes, it works that way," Frank told her. "That's why it took me so long to get some of them written. Sometimes the words did not come."

"Dad, I am so sorry I gave you such a hard time about you writing your letters," Emma said, shaking her head sadly. "I had no idea."

"It's okay," Dad said with a smile.

"I will never give you a hard time ever again," Emma promised.

"Emma, did you enjoy writing them?" Frank asked her.

"I did, but I don't think it's my thing," she told him honestly. "I don't have the patience for it and besides God has been giving me other ways to give back which I am enjoying a lot better."

A knock on the door, "Miss Emma can we go outside and play?"

"Sure, let me get my coat," she said, and Emma and the boys made their way outside.

It was a beautiful morning with the snow coming down. Emma got an idea and texted Sam to see if he wanted to come over and join in on the fun.

"Hi, what are we doing?" Sam asked.

"We're trying to build a fort, but we could use some help," Emma told him. "Do you mind?"

"Not at all," Sam said.

"Good you build, I need a cup of hot chocolate," Emma said with a smile. "I'll be back. Oh, by the way, Josh's mom had a baby girl last night."

"That's great, we need to get her something," Sam said.

"I know, Mom and I are going over this afternoon after we shop," Emma told him as she headed in the door.

While Emma was inside getting her hot chocolate, she received another text, but this time it was from Jennifer asking her how it was going. Emma made her way back outside and took a couple of pictures and sent them to Jennifer. The only thing she said was we're having fun and Stacey had a baby girl.

A couple of seconds later, Emma's phone rang, "I thought she was having a boy?"

"I did, too," Emma told Jennifer. "Mom and I are heading over this afternoon. I'll send you a picture. Are you having fun?"

"Emma, we are. After breakfast, we're going Christmas shopping," Jennifer said excitedly. "Thank you so much for this, I can never thank you enough."

"Jenn, it's my pleasure. You deserve this," Emma said. "Hey, I got to go, the fort is almost done. Have fun!"

"You, too," Jennifer said. "Thanks again."

Emma made her way outside to see an interesting looking fort.

"Miss Emma, what do you think?" Jack asked her.

"I think you boys did great, but it's missing something," Emma said as she picked up some snow and threw the first of many snowballs at Sam.

The fight was on. After a while, the boys got tired and they all went inside for hot chocolate. Mary and James came over for lunch and then headed out to do some last-minute Christmas shopping.

After lunch, Emma and Ruth made their way to the hospital after stopping to pick up a baby gift. Seeing her baby girl made Emma smile.

"She's beautiful, what's her name?" Emma asked.

"Emma Theresa," Stacey told them. "Emma after you and Theresa after my mom."

Emma could not believe it, "You named her after me?"

"Yes, Josh insisted and we agreed," Stacey said with a smile.

Emma looked down at her namesake, kissed the top of her-head, handed her back to Stacey, and made her way to Josh who was watching a movie on his I Pad.

Kneeling down, she said, "Josh, you wanted to name your sister after me?"

"Yeah," he said and smiled.

"Josh, you just gave me the best Christmas present!" Emma told him.

"It's not Christmas yet, Miss Emma," Josh told her.

"I know but trust me, this is the best Christmas gift!" Emma told him. "Thank you, Josh."

Emma could not help but stare at Emma Theresa.

"She's right, you are an angel, Emma," Ruth told her.

"No, I'm not. I just enjoy helping others," Emma said.

"You have a gift of serving," Ruth told her.

"Mom, there is something I need to tell you," and Emma told her Mom about all of the tasks God had given her, what she had to do the week before Christmas, and what she had done already, like taking Mrs. Tracey Christmas shopping and having lunch with her.

"I wrote Mr. Pretzel a thank you note for sending you and Dad that note many years ago on Christmas Eve, and I sent him a bouquet of yellow roses which was his wife's favorite color," Emma told her mom.

"I invited Mr. Sendler over for Christmas dinner and I am going to help out in the nursery at church after the holidays," Emma said, finally finished.

"Are you sure you have time for all of this?" Ruth asked her.

"I am, it's what God wants me to do," Emma told her confidently.

"Well, I'm proud of you," Ruth said and gave her a big hug.

"Thanks, Mom," Emma said with a smile.

The week before Christmas, Emma was busier than she thought imaginable, but it was well worth it. Between working at the soup kitchen with her parents and babysitting Josh and Emma Theresa and spending time with Sam, this was the best Christmas ever.

"Emma, you need to slow down, you look exhausted," Sam told her.

"I'm okay, tomorrow is Christmas Eve and every task that God has given me is almost complete," Emma told him. "There is only one thing left to do and I am hoping to have it done by tomorrow."

"What is it, maybe I can help," Sam offered.

"Thanks, Sam, I appreciate it, but this one I have to do myself," Emma smiled.

"Well, can you at least tell me what you're working on?" Sam asked.

"No, but I will let you know when it's done, I promise," Emma told him.

Sam could see that this last task was starting to worry Emma.

"So, do you want to know what I got you for Christmas?" Sam asked her.

"You bought me a gift?" Emma asked.

"Of course, I did," Sam told her.

"You did not have to," Emma smiled.

"Yes, I did! It's Christmas," Sam said. "And I'm sure you bought me something, too."

"How do you know that?" she asked him.

"Emma, that's the kind of person you are," Sam said with a smile. "You think of everyone, even my parents."

"Well, I had to get them something," she admitted.

"You still have not told me what you got them," Sam reminded her.

"And you are not going to know until tomorrow night, either," she told him firmly.

"You are going to church with us tomorrow night, aren't you?" Emma asked him.

"Yes, we wouldn't miss it," Sam assured her. "Is your Mom enjoying her table?"

"She loves it," Emma assured him. "Your Mom did a great job, I'll never forget the look on Mom's face when she came home and found her dining room table decorated for Christmas."

"Your Dad did a great job keeping her gone for that long," Sam laughed.

"I know, I am sure it wasn't easy," Emma laughed as well.

"Emma, there is something we need to talk about," Sam told her.

"Sam, can it wait until tomorrow?" she asked him. "I'm so tired, I can barely keep my eyes open."

"Sure," Sam said. "Come on, let's get you home."

Emma wasn't kidding when she said she was exhausted. She started drifting off to sleep on the way home.

"Emma, we're here," Sam said, gently waking her up.

"I'm sorry, Sam. I didn't mean to fall asleep," Emma apologized.

"It's okay," Sam smiled. "Let's get you inside."

Sam took her hand and helped her into her condo.

"Good night, Sam," Emma said and kissed him on the cheek.

"Good night, Emma. See you tomorrow," Sam said as he waved goodbye and drove off in his truck.

Emma was exhausted and her last task was taking its toll on her. Emma went straight to bed praying that the words would come one last time.

Christmas Eve morning Emma woke up feeling refreshed. She got her coffee and made her way to her window seat. With her Dad's pen, she wrote her very last Christmas Letter. As the words came, tears filled her eyes and a smile came to her face.

Later that afternoon, with all of her gifts wrapped, Emma made her way to her parents' house. She greeted Ben, Cathy, her nephews, and her parents.

Her Mom pulled her aside and asked, "Are you alright?"

"I'm fine, everything is done," Emma told her with a smile.

"Good, now we need to hurry," Ruth said. "Everyone, time for church, get your coats."

"Dad, let me help you," Emma said as her dad struggled to get his heavy coat over his cast.

"Thanks, Emma," he told her with a smile.

When they reached church, Emma and her Mom walked on each side of her Dad so he would not fall.

"I think I can manage, ladies," he told them realizing what they were doing.

"We are not taking any chances," Ruth said firmly.

"Hey, Dad," Ben yelled. "You want to race?"

Everybody laughed, but Ruth.

"Not funny," Ruth said.

"Oh, Mom, I was only kidding," Ben told her.

"Benjamin, behave yourself," Ruth told him firmly.

Emma smiled when she walked in and found Sam waiting for her.

"My parents saved us all seats," Sam told them. "They're up in front with Jennifer and her family."

"Merry Christmas, Emma," Sam said giving her a big smile.

"Merry Christmas, Sam," she responded as she took his arm and they made their way up the aisle.

Listening to the choir made Emma smile. They had the best choir in town.

After the service, Emma spoke to Jennifer who looked refreshed.

"Hi, what day are you free next week?" Emma asked.

"I don't have any plans, why?" Jennifer asked her.

"Keep a day open for me, okay?" Emma asked her friend.

"I will," Jenn told her. "Just let me know which day."

"Merry Christmas, Jenn."

"Merry Christmas, Emma."

As everyone made their way to Emma's parents' house for dinner, Emma heard that "angel" song[2] on the radio once again and a smile came to her face. Now she knew for sure God had sent that song for her every time she had gotten in her car. The words now carried an extra special meaning for her.[3]

As they all got out of their cars and walked toward the house, Sam stopped Emma, "Can we talk a minute, Emma?"

"Sure, Sam," Emma smiled up at him.

"I have something for you," he said, pulling some mistletoe from his pocket.

"What am I supposed to do with that?" she asked, coyly.

"If you don't know, we have a problem," Sam said with a smile.

Emma reached up and kissed Sam for the first time.

---

2 "Somebody's Angel," sung by Mandissa

3 Album: It's Christmas (Christmas Angel Edition)

"Now, put that back in your pocket for later," she smiled, then turned and went inside grinning.

After dinner, and after all of the presents were unwrapped, Emma went and placed the last letter on her Dad's desk along with his special pen.

"We're going to head out," she yelled to her Mom and Dad. "And Dad, I left something on your desk."

"What is it?" he asked, but Emma just smiled and winked and headed out the door.

Frank walked into his office finding an envelope and his pen. Opening the envelope Frank took out a Christmas Letter from his daughter. With tears in his eyes, he read his very first Christmas Letter.

One Year Later

Christmas Eve

"Do you have the Christmas Letters?" Sam asked.

"Honey, you have asked twice now," Emma laughed. "I have them, don't worry!

Hugging his wife, he laughed, "I'm was just checking."

"You would think that after six months of marriage, my husband would know that I am very organized," Emma said.

"Now where is my purse?" she asked, and everyone laughed.

"Emma, honey, wait until you're married fifty years. It does get easier," James laughed.

"Let's go or we'll be late," Mary encouraged them.

"Are you sure you don't want to walk?" Sam asked them. "It's just across the road."

"Absolute not!" Mary said. "Have you seen Emma's and my shoes? We are not walking in snow in these."

"Now Sam, take your wife to the car," his mother told him.

"Yes, Mother," he replied with a grin.

"James are all of the packages in the car?" Mary asked her husband.

"No, Sam, Frank, and I brought them over earlier," James reminded her.

"Oh yes, I remember," Mary said, putting her coat on.

Backing out of the driveway and turning into her parents' driveway seemed silly, but with ice, nobody was about to take the short walk for granted.

"Want to skate up the driveway?" Sam asked, as he walked around and helped his wife out of the car.

"Not funny," Emma said trying not to laugh.

"How about a race up to the front door?" Sam teased.

"Samuel, if your wife falls, you will be dealing with me," Mary threatened.

"Yes, Mother," Sam told her. "I was just kidding."

Making their way into the house and seeing Ruth's table all decorated thanks to Mary, made Emma smile.

"Emma, can you go get your Dad?" Ruth asked her. "He's in his office."

"Sure," Emma said.

Knocking on the door, she poked her head in and said, "Dad, Mom's looking for you."

"I'll be there in a minute, Emma," her Dad said with a smile. "Thanks for helping me the Letters this year. Addressing the envelopes and helping me figure out who needed to hear from me this year really helped."

"We make a pretty good team," Emma said, smiling at her Dad.

"Yes, we do," Frank smiled. "And we got to spend a lot of time together."

"And you got to go Christmas shopping with Mom," Emma added.

"I can't tell you the last time your Mom and I Christmas shopped together," her Dad said. "More importantly, no one got hurt or injured this year!"

"Amen for that," Emma agreed.

"Emma?" Sam knocked. "It's time."

"It's time for what?" her Dad asked.

"It's time for all of us to open our Christmas Letters," Emma smiled.

"That was a great idea, Emma," Frank told her.

"Thanks, Dad," she said. "I was just thinking, why should only our friends get Christmas Letters this year."

"Well, picking names and writing a letter to someone in the family was a great idea!" Frank told her.

With all of them sitting around the living room, Sam asked, "So, who should go first?"

"Mom and Dad, I think you should go first," Emma said, smiling at her husband. "In fact, why don't you open yours together?"

Emma once again looked up and whispered, "You got this right?"

Dear Mom,
Merry Christmas!
How would you feel about being called Grandma
when your grandchild arrives?
Love,
Emma

Dear Dad,
Merry Christmas!
How would you feel about being called Grandpa
when your grandchild arrives?
Love,
Emma

CPSIA information can be obtained
at www.ICGtesting.com
Printed in the USA
LVHW04s1931190518
577828LV00001B/3/P

9 781545 629284